THIEF OF PARADISE

THIEF OF PARADISE

by

Shirley F. Ricks

1stBooks - rev. 02/25/00

About the Book

Roman justice was harsh, but it was not blind. The man tried and executed as a thief was indeed a thief. But *what* did he steal? It must have been unusual. For as he died, Christ himself promised him Paradise!

Who was this strange man known by tradition only as "Dismas"? No accolades of righteousness were ever ascribed to him. There is only brief mention made of him in the New Testament. Yet, since the first icons appeared in the Orthodox Churches, his own has been revered the world over.

Perhaps he was much like some of us. Courageous on occasion, ever so foolish on love, certainly the follower of Wandering Star, he found his destiny in the deserts of Palestine. Part fact, largely fiction, this is the story of the Thief of Paradise.

CHAPTER ONE

Portia twisted sideways and leaned toward the Centurion who lounged on the couch next to hers. The music, bouncing along in rhythmic beat, together with the high-pitched voices of the party, had drowned his voice, even though she had seen his lips moving and a smile turning up the corners of his mouth. He, in turn, bent toward her at the same moment. Thus it was that his eyes caught sight of her firm breasts riding up from the confines of her gown like acorns ready to shed their shells. His breath caught in his throat; her delicious fragrance filled his nostrils, and his head swam. Now that she was closer to Centurion Sinstra and comfortable, her gown resumed its proper drape just as her innocent and friendly eyes looked directly into Partheus Sinstra's burning gaze. Her big violet eyes widened in surprise while her smile froze on her face. Suddenly she was aware of a wave of heat sweeping up and across her face while a strange tingle spread across her thighs. Her throat closed, and she gasped. From somewhere nearby, startlingly close and almost smothered by the party noise, there came a soft moan. Grateful for the interruption, she forced her eyes to look at the next table and directly at her friend, Lady Titus, who was leaning intimately close to a handsome Centurion. They were oblivious to all else. What was happening to everyone?

Portia lowered her eyes, grasped her wine goblet, and stared into the swirling liquid. Had someone doped the wine? Absurd thought! Striving for composure, she considered her unexpected reaction to the burning expression of the Centurion's gaze and her own physical response.

There was no denying her response to his look. Her mind raced to sort out these feelings, but she could get no farther than to realize that these new emotions were "out of bounds", and she was enchanted with curiosity. It was so delightful and deliciously intriguing! She must remember who she was and who he was. And there _was_ Alexander!

1

Her face cooled. When she could finally breathe again, she turned toward him.

"I'm sorry, Partheus. I didn't hear what you just said. It is so <u>noisy</u> in the garden!"

Secretly, to her own private dismay, she realized perverse pleasure in using his first name. Feeling the pull of his eyes, she didn't want to resist it! Tentatively and slowly, she raised her gaze to meet his. This time, there was nothing tentative or gentle in the roar of emotion sweeping through her. She began to tremble and could not stop.

Partheus savored her slip from decorum. He noticed her tremor and was aware, as any man would be that his arousal was answered by her own. His voice thickened as he answered:

"Nothing of importance, Portia. I had just observed that Lady Titus seems to have become inordinately pleased with her escort of the evening."

Partheus was aware of the irony of his words, and his eyes locked with Portia's. Still, the words provided their own shock therapy. Both looked simultaneously at the scene at the next table and realized that they had intruded upon a scene of intimacy. Lady and Centurion were entwined and kissing hungrily, oblivious to anything and anyone around them.

Embarrassed, Partheus cleared his throat and said quietly,

"Let's hope that news of this pleasantry will not reach the ears of Senator Titus when he returns."

Portia nodded her agreement, downed the last of her wine, then put her goblet down with a thud. She was surprised with her own behavior. What had come over everyone and herself as well?

Suddenly, the word "Tribune" seemed to ring through Sinstra`s mind. `Tribune' indeed! He stared down at Portia`s golden head still bent over her goblet. So lovely. So enticing. So forbidden! The impossibility of even a future dalliance into such an ecstatic abyss swept over him. Desire subsided but slowly. His fingers toyed with his own goblet. A surge of protectiveness replaced desire. Bone-deep discipline and many years of loyalty to the Tribune won out, and Partheus experienced a reluctant relief.

"Lady Gaius, may I escort you to your quarters?"

"An excellent idea, Centurion!" Portia's voice was light and high, almost shrill with excitement and relief.

They walked briskly through the riotous garden party next to the portico of the Praetorium, up the stairs leading to the level of the Tribune's Office, and upward still to the private entrance of the Gaius' living quarters.

The cool breeze had begun to clear the wine's fuzz from their heads, though there remained the lingering mystique of the forbidden intimacy of the earlier moment. His hand on her arm, assisting her up the stairs, was strong but not possessive. His thoughts were of admiration, while hers were deeply grateful. They stopped before the door of the apartment, and Partheus dropped his arm. Deliberately, her fingers grasped his, ever so gently, with a gentle and friendly squeeze. She looked up and smiled, a little wistfully he thought.

"Thank you, Partheus, for your strength and valor, both of which my husband would understand and resent deeply. I too thank you, though for so much more that I'm sure you understand."

Knowing that more words could either ruin the moment or get him into trouble, Partheus lifted her hand and kissed her fingers lightly.

"Lady Gaius, thank you for a cherished moment. Good night." Both knew that, for them, it was also good-bye.

On the elevated portico adjacent to his private office in the Praetorium, the big man stood with hands clasped behind his back and surveyed the scene below. Rome, a sparkling jewel of marble set in gold in the sunlight of the day, was sheer fairyland at night. This night, the start of the Fall Season, was gloriously beautiful. Tribune Alexander Gaius, from his splendid vantage point, let his black eyes dart appreciatively over this evening's display of enchantment in The City of The Gods. From this spot behind the junction of Anzio and Martian Aqueducts, one could see the beginning flicker of torchlights. They spread upward, then over the Quirinal and Viminal Hills, threading their way ultimately to the far reaches of the city wrapped around by the Servian Wall. In their light glowed a thousand gardens bedecked with flowers and lilting music of softly-strummed lyres.

Beautiful? Yes. But here, directly above the garden which separated this side from the Praetorium barracks, there was a third dimension to the party in progress. To the eye, there was the same beauty. To the ear, the same sounds of music, though the sound of human voices in celebration distorted the beauty. Smell was the third dimension, "smell" as differing from "fragrance." Gaius' beaked nose wrinkled in distaste of the heterologous smells of steaming platters of food mixing with nauseous sweetness of thousands of flowers.

With a snort, he turned his back on the festivity below and retreated to the seclusion of his office. His aging stomach could no longer tolerate intemperance of either food or wine; surely not both. Nor had he been able to drink socially without the possibility of image-threatening drunkenness.

His crippled stride had carried him back into the office and to the huge document-laden table where he sank into the great chair, and for the moment, the tight pain in his chest occupied his attention. His timing was such that he missed seeing Portia and Partheus climbing the stairs to the apartment in such proximity that he might easily have been greatly disturbed. Fortunately, he was spared the anguish of an erroneous conclusion.

For a moment, he stared at the scrolls demanding his attention. The stack never got any smaller. Idly, he considered the matter of parties. Did he really hate them? Well, not the parties themselves, but he loathed the effect. Every invitation filled him with dread. Was it because of Portia? He recalled the vision of her smiling at him from the doorway this very night and then whirling prettily to join her escort, Centurion Sinstra. His fingernails dug into his palms as he recalled how the stolla had drifted to one side, revealing a perky breast swelling from the low-cut gown. And the drape of her gown flowed sensuously over her curved, youthful bottom. Jealous anger still stirred within him as recalled men's ill-concealed expressions of desire wherever they appeared together.

Perhaps his jealousy was understandable. But why was it, he wondered, that just lately she would return their smiles with one of her own? Dimpled and innocent to be sure but accompanying that smile was an almost imperceptible little skip and barely audible girlish chuckle..wasn't it just like that when his own flirtation began? Come to think of it, she didn't act like that with him any more. Was he no longer attractive to her? Was his age showing, the magic gone? When was it that her eyes had cooled, and she became indifferent to his connubial advances? His duties had obscured the passage of time; but as he thought about it, a pattern of behavior emerged.

The change had begun with her foolish chatter about starting a family! Not telling her of his sterility before marriage might have reflected badly upon his virility, and confessing it now just seemed unnecessary. But that <u>was</u> when it all started, if he just told her the truth, just <u>out</u> with it! After all, she was just a woman, though a pretty one at that. That was the beginning of it. He was simply afraid of losing her because of their age difference. Then, what if his men laughed behind his back, snickering because he was not only too crippled to soldier but too elderly for sexual prowess as well?

Age? Nonsense! Stretching his arms with their graceful musculature out in front of him and flexing the long, supple hands, he felt the resurgence of youth.   In the act, his gaze fell upon the Emperor's Ring on the third finger, right hand. That had been awarded to him commemorative of "Excellence of Valor" at the Battle of The Danube. No one mentioned his age then.

He stretched luxuriously, winced at the stiffness of his back and the cramp that grabbed his bad leg. It was a silly waste of time, thinking foolish thoughts about age. He wasn't <u>that</u> old! With a grunt, he leaned forward and picked up the scroll on the top of the pile to open it. And all thoughts, idle or otherwise, fled as he began to read.

Then his eyes burned, and an ache filled his chest. He lowered the papyrus and stared into space, into the Past. So long, long ago that day, that last day of real youth, when the two of them, he and Apollus, had basked in the Sun and talked for hours. They had always been great friends, but each knew that there would be a difference in their relationship after that day.

Both had begun their careers as senators. Then, Apollus Voltanus was appointed Legatus with Gaius immediately under him as Commanding Tribune, heady new assignments for both of them. The intimacy of friendship precluded laxity with either; and probably because of each determining to excel in the other's esteem, each was outstanding. Ambition had been heady wine through the years, but it had taken its toll.

He stood and paced the floor with his gimpy lope, pondering the significance of what he had just read. Voltanus requested a favor rather than requiring of him obedience to an order. The Legate was dying, the letter said, though the writer did not state the cause. The matter at hand, it seemed, concerned a young man named Dismas, a Greek, who had been in the Voltanus household since boyhood. With mention of him, Gaius remembered him ever so vividly on that momentous day of The Battle of The Danube.

When he had finished the letter, he settled back easily into his chair, and his voice rumbled into the empty room:

"We'll take care of that lad, Old Friend. Better than you can ask..yes, better than you can imagine." While these thoughts were still on his mind, he picked up pen and papyrus and wrote his reply. His letter began with "Apollus, Old Friend" and continued with rare warmth until it was a fat packet, sealed and waiting for a messenger. Another more tersely stated communication was addressed to the border garrison of the Third Legion.

Having finished the letters, he recalled the crazy yarn that he had spun for Portia. A craggy smile moved his mouth, and his shoulders shook with an amused chuckle. No wise person would ever tell a woman of battles and of their horror. So, when he told her of the Greek who had saved his life, a tale of near-tragedy which ended in triumph, it had been with tongue in cheek and outrageous humor. In its fictionalized version, The Bugler had appeared like a gladiator gone amok at a garden party! Portia trilled with laughter and promptly created a legend of all her own, still asking for the story over and over again. She had seemed utterly entranced with the idea of The Bugler as make-believe hero. As a matter of fact, thinking back on it, even he had begun to think of The Bugler as imaginary until Voltanus' letter arrived.

He stood again now. His body was stiff, and his leg hurt. He resented the limp as he crossed to the door and snuffed out the light. It was later than he would have thought. Climbing slowly to his apartment, he found himself thinking of Dismas, recalling his appearance when he, Gaius, had left the border and returned to Rome.

"I've missed that scrappy bugler," he mused. "I wonder if he's changed and whether he'll be surprised with my decision." He continued talking softly to himself as he opened the door to his apartment and concluded with:

"I wonder whether he knows of Apollus." With that, he shrugged and closed the door.

Life in the border garrison could be tedious. But for the Roman Auxiliary, it was an arduous routine of running, calisthenics, and drill with the sword. Free time was a rarity which all welcomed and most used to enjoy wine and the sweet pleasure of the women who were seldom far from the fort. Dismas loved the idea but feared the entanglement.

He sat back against the wooden racks of the steam room and watched the swirling eddies of vapor dance over the hot coals. He edged his way over the slippery tiles to the shower, rinsed off the salt and sweat, and picked up a towel to dry his eyes briefly before diving into the pool.

The shock of the cold water took his breath away and numbed him briefly. Then, as he surfaced, exhilaration took over. Wonderful! It was great to be alive! He began his daily routine of swimming laps back and forth across the pool and was well into the rhythm of his strokes when he heard his name being called. He stopped, treading water to determine the source. Then he heard it clearly,

"Dismas...Dismas of Siracusa!"

"Yes, I am he. What is it?"

"Tribune Marius has directed me to tell you to dress and report to him at once. You have an assignment."

I'll be there as soon as I can dress," he answered. A sense of uneasiness came over him. What or who could direct him to report at once when he was off duty?

Lifting himself smoothly from the pool, he splashed through a quick shower and hurried to the barracks to put on a clean uniform before reporting to the Tribune. He walked through the long shadows of early morning and suspected that he would shiver if there were time.

"You are Dismas?" the guard on duty asked.

"Yes."

"Follow me." The guard walked briskly ahead of him, knocked briefly Dismas at the door, and then entered.

"Auxiliary of Siracusa is reporting in, Sir."

Tribune Marius looked up, returned the guard's salute casually, and then looked over the Auxiliary with obvious curiosity.

"So you're the man," he grunted.

"Sir?"

"You have orders here, sent to me directly from the Commanding Tribune in Rome, Alexander Gaius. There is no explanation. You are to report to him at once."

Marius stopped and looked at Dismas, obviously waiting for some answer to the implied question of "why?" When none was forthcoming, he continued:

"Very well. Stand at ease. Here are your orders."

While the Auxiliary stared dumbly at the blunt script of Gaius' penmanship, Marius turned and walked back to his desk.

"While you were getting over here, I had a horse saddled for you. Two men were sent to the barracks to round up your things and pack them, while yet another put enough nuts and grain together for your trip. It's all right here, and you will depart at once. You are to report directly to Tribune Alexander Gaius when you arrive, and you should be there within two days. Have you any questions?"

"None. Thank you for the horse and for the provisions. Goodbye, Sir." He saluted crisply and turned to leave.

Tribune Marius frowned in the suspicion that Dismas knew a lot more than he was telling.

Tired and hungry, Dismas arrived at the great garrison gate in Rome shortly after dawn on the third day. He presented his orders, and the gates swung open for his passage.

The guard took his orders, read them with interest, and then spoke with unusual kindness:

"The Tribune will not be in his office for another hour. Why not take time for a visit to the Baths and have breakfast before you report in? I'm sure he'll approve." He smiled, then summoned an orderly to take his horse to the stables. His directions to the Baths were easily followed, and Dismas was soon enjoying an invigorating swim.

Then, breakfast followed, and with the Sun having risen toward midmorning, he reported to the senior Auxiliary in Tribune Gaius' Office.

He stepped into the office, extended his orders crisply to the surprised older man and announced:

"Auxiliary Dismas of Siracusa reporting for duty in accordance with these orders!"

Barely able to hide his amusement, Gaius senior clerk said:

"Standby, Auxiliary, until I tell Tribune Gaius that you have arrived." With that, he stepped into the inner office, and Dismas heard a buzz of voices. Then,

"Step in, Auxiliary. The Tribune will see you now."

Walking through the door, Dismas halted and stood at attention before the long table where Gaius sat, ostensibly leafing through the scrolls before him. Presently, he looked up and surveyed carefully the handsome young man standing so stiffly before him. Yes, The Bugler of The Past, as he remembered him, was still there; but time and military seasoning had broadened his shoulders and hardened him into a formidable Roman soldier. Oh, Zeus! To be young again!

"Stand easy, Hornblower!' Gaius rumbled. A smile eased his stern features as he continued:

"Tell me. Was your journey without event?"

"Yes, Sir." Dismas felt the urge to smile with having been addressed as `Hornblower', but caution restrained him until he knew more of his situation.

"Good. It makes for a smooth beginning."

The Tribune sat back in his chair, stared briefly at the ceiling, then back at the young man before him.

"Before I set about changing your life and telling you of your future, I want to dig into your memory, as it were, and ask some questions to clear up my recollections."

"Sir?"

"Well, it's this way. I know that you saved my life. That much is clear. But the details are hazy. Can you help me with this?"

"Yes, Sir, I think I can. I remember clearly the day and the events to a point, that is, to the point at which I was hit on the head. Then things are somewhat blurred."

"What do you recall?"

"Well, the battle seemed to be going much as planned. And then there was chaos and the unexpected. Even as I put my bugle to my lips to sound your command, I saw your horse go down, pinning you under him. An arrow slammed into my left shoulder; and, at the same time, a madman on foot charged toward you with his sword upraised to cut off your head, I suspect. I had spurred my horse to run him down when another arrow hit my helmet and toppled me from the saddle. I found myself rolling toward that barbarian, feeling unable to stop him and knowing that I was probably going to be too late."

"Yes, that's the way it was. I thought we were both dead."

"Then, I rolled to my feet," Dismas continued, "and saw that the swordsman had paused to lift his blade higher for the extra leverage for just one final blow. I kicked his arm as it came down, and the sword flew through the air. I caught it. He charged me then, not seeing the sword in my hand, and dropped his shoulder to flatten me. The edge of the sword sliced into his neck, and his momentum did the rest. His body did knock me down. And when I pushed it off, I saw that it had no head. I looked for you, saw that you were alive, but I couldn't get to you. I was drifting then and supposed that I was dying. There was this strange peace, and I knew that I would die a Roman Soldier. That's all I recall."

Gaius was entranced.

"Strange. Why would you think about `dying a Roman Soldier'? Why would that matter?"

"I would be free."

"Does it matter at death whether you're free?"

Dismas blinked, brought his gaze back to the Tribune, and wondered whether he could understand.

"Yes, Commander. Freedom always matters. Even then no Roman ever dies a slave, a servant, or even an Auxiliary."

The silence was awkward.

"Ah, yes, I see."

Gaius did not understand, of course, but he did know in a moment that the boy had become a man, a man with thoughts that very easily could be his undoing. Time to change the subject.

"Have you been informed that the Legate Augustus Apollus Voltanus is gravely ill?"

"No, Sir."

"I am sorry. This is not the easiest way for you to learn that he is dying. We don't know when that will be, of course; nor do we know the cause of his illness."

Gaius lowered his eyes to the document-laden table, giving Dismas time to absorb the news while he himself sought out the best way to say the words that would change this man's life.

"In this packet in which the news came to me, there was his personal request that I improve your status in whatever way that I deemed feasible. He berated himself for having been so lax as not to have adopted you legally as had been his intent all along. You see, to him, you were his son in every way, and the adoption process was a bothersome thing. Therefore, as he requested, you will bear his surname and be known as Cassius Demetrius Voltanus." Gaius paused.

"How wonderfully kind. Demetrius was his son's name before he died." The Auxiliary's eyes misted. He swallowed, but the lump was still there.

Gaius continued.

"Now more good news. He knew, of course, that I have been ordered to Palestine; and, since he wants you to be with me, we have to do a little more than just change your name."

He glanced over at Dismas.

"Therefore, by the Imperium of My Office, vested in me by order of the Emperor of Rome, I appoint you from this time forward to be a Citizen of Rome! You would, of course, have received your citizenship in due course when you retire from the Auxiliary."

Gaius, unaccustomed to emotion in the presence of other men, found himself struggling. But he continued:

"As a Roman Citizen in service to The Emperor, your rank will be Centurion. Your duties will be those of my assistant, though," he chuckled, ~I doubt that we will need your bugle."

Dismas, now Cassius Voltanus, was speechless. The Tribune reached down to the end of the great table and picked up a leather bag.

"Your new uniform..insignia, tunic, sandals, et cetera.. all are in this bag, and you will change into them now in that small dressing room at the end of my office."

He smiled and added: "Congratulations, Centurion!"

Cassius saluted, took the bag, then turned as with an after-thought:

"When I have changed, where do I go? And I know nothing of being a Centurion; can anyone help me?"

"Oh, yes. Centurion Partheus Sinstra is waiting for you. I have ordered him to train you in matters of military protocol and bearing as well as in the specific duties that go with your position. Learn as much as you can as quickly as you can, because we must leave shortly to visit your father,,hopefully before he dies. Have you any more questions?"

"No, Sir."

"You are dismissed."

Cassius saluted again, turned smartly, and strode from the room. Once in the welcome confines of the small dressing room, he slipped on the tunic and began to fumble with the insignia.

"Are you ready yet, Centurion?"

Cassius peered out the door.

"Will you help me, Centurion Sinstra? I have no idea of how this goes together."

Sinstra laughed quietly, remembering his own confusion when he was commissioned, though he had the benefit of the outfitter's counsel.

"Yes, my friend, we will put you together."

In a short time, the insignia was in place and Cassius was in his newly-acquired uniform.

"What do you think I should do with this?" Cassius asked.

Sinstra took the Auxiliary's plain tunic from his hand and dumped it without comment into the other rubbish of the garrison.

"I don't know where you came from, Cassius Voltanus, but I suspect that you have just begun to get where you're going! Meanwhile, we'll get you comfortable in your living quarters. The Tribune has told me nothing of you except that you will need intense training in horsemanship and the rudiments of Officer's Etiquette. It will be my pleasure to show you. Come with me. Welcome to the Glories of Rome!"

CHAPTER TWO

The perfume of the bath. the tickle of bubbles under her chin, the water's languorous warmth..all invited Portia to stretch out beneath the foam and consider the dalliance of the night before. As she savored the memory, she found herself tingling again with the thoughts of just what could have happened. What fun!

And imagine Nora and that handsome Centurion! He couldn't compare, of course, with Partheus. And Alexander? Well, he would be well justified to one of his jealous tantrums if he even suspected what she was thinking! Her thoughts stuttered and froze, reacting to the instantaneous thrill that grabbed at her middle with the thought. Her eyes widened, remembering Partheus` hot eyes looking down at her. Beneath the foam, feeling hidden and safe, she closed her eyes and imagined that she felt again Sinstra's touch on her hand, then her arm, and his lips as they kissed her fingers. She felt the delicious flush of warmth. Her heart pounded for no good reason, and even breathing deeply still left her feeling peculiarly giddy. Thank goodness that neither Sinstra nor Gaius would ever know how she felt! She knew that she should just ignore the enticing tremble of her limbs. But why? Did Lady Titus feel like this, or maybe even better? She enjoyed her caprice in fantasy and opened her hands so that her fingers fumbled with bouquets of bubbles. Captive now of her own imagination, her mind pushed her into sensuous fantasy with Partheus' face where Alexander 's should have been. Her lips softened, and her eyes drooped.

She sighed aloud, and the sound startled her. She sat up with a gasp. What kind of fool was she? That Partheus bit was over! She felt dreadfully naughty! Almost dutifully she rose, shivering. She snatched the great yellow towel and wrapped her shining nakedness into it. There. That was better. Now she could face some facts. She liked that excitement! And she had never felt anything like that with Alex.

15

Her affection for Alex was akin to her feeling for her father. Peculiarly, intimacy with Alex had always seemed a bit wrong, almost incestuous; and she felt no pleasure in his touch. Strange. Why, she wondered?

Oh well..she alone knew her thoughts. Hugging her secret to herself, she giggled a little and ran over to a big pillow directly in the shaft of sun coming through the archway. She cuddled down into its center and felt the pull of drowsiness. As she began to doze, she felt safe remembering, in spite of daydreaming, that last night was over , and Partheus Sinstra had been sane enough for both of them. At least, if she had sense enough to realize that the danger had been put behind her, she should have been wise enough to remember who she was and act accordingly! She sighed and slipped into sleep.

Perhaps it was a scuff on the floor or a breeze that woke her, and her eyes opened slowly to gaze at a pair of male feet and legs beside her nest. Her eyes moved swiftly up to the edge of the tunic..a familiar one. Gaius' smiling face looked down at her.

"Hello, my sleepy kitten," his big voice rumbled gently.

Laughing, Portia stretched within her yellow cocoon, and she shook her finger at him in mock scolding:

"How dare you expose me as being so lazy, Mr. Tribune? And, of course, that reminds me what are you doing out of your office?"

They both laughed.

"Just spying on my wife if anyone should ask."

"Will she tolerate that, Lofty Commander?"

"Possibly not. I suppose that I'd better leave before I find myself in deep trouble." He feigned embarrassment and turned to go. The small basket that he was holding wobbled, and she saw it for the first time.

"What is that?" she asked as one white arm snaked out of the towel, and one nail-lacquered finger pointed to the basket.

"Oh, I almost forgot. My excuse for being here, of course! I was bringing the invitations to you that you wanted to address and send out you know, invitations to our farewell banquet in three weeks."

Portia stretched and yawned. Her top half sprouted from the

towel.

"Ahhh.." In an instant, Alex had dropped the basket, bent to scoop her up in his arms, and held her close. His lips pressed against her breasts, and his sprouting beard rubbed across them. She pulled away.

"Ouch! Alex, you're so rough!"

"Sorry. I didn't mean to be." And his lips sought hers.

As she surrendered her lips, she wondered just why it was that Alex always seemed to annoy her in these times of physical attention. Why, only an hour ago, just the thought of Partheus doing the same thing had practically thrown her into a fit! Ticking off this sojourn of thought presented Alex with nothing more than her flaccid passivity. As always, he was stopped cold with the patient smile and the pliant but indifferent response. He rubbed his cheek and was startled with the growth of beard that was there. He sat her down gently, wrapped the towel securely around her again, and set the basket of invitations on a nearby table.

"Goodbye, Kitten. I want to get back to the office. See you later."

Portia watched him leave and noted the dejected droop of his shoulders. He was such a dear man and so good to her, and they <u>did</u> get along famously for the most part. It was just this physical bit that she found annoying. She sighed and moved languidly toward the dressing room. The towel unwound itself as she moved, and her hand closed on one of its corners. She resembled a pale bird with yellow tail-feathers behind.

Her disquiet dissipated with the work of getting the invitations out. Later, she gave the basket to Lea, her maidservant, and instructed her to give them to Julian for delivery.

Portia strolled from the room onto the bedroom balcony which overlooked the Garrison Garden where last night's party had provided so much excitement. Looking past the Garrison toward the city stretching away beyond her vision, she smiled. It was a beautiful place, Rome, but surely there was more to the world than this! Palestine, for instance, would surely offer more than parties. She was hopelessly sick of parties. She laughed softly to herself as she recalled her girlhood ideas that Rome was marvelous, an escape with glitter. Glitter it had, to be sure, but she learned that with her country upbringing, she could never be a "city girl". Two more weeks here and two more parties. She had already decided just yesterday that she would buy no more gowns for either party; she had a room full! She would make her decision on the gowns to wear and spend the rest of the time packing her clothes and jewelry for Palestine.

And the gowns that she didn't want, she decided to leave for the garrison servants. She went back into the big, beautiful room that was hers, entered the alcove where her clothes hung, and began to sort through. Each garment brought forth memories. One gown which she had brought with her from Alba suddenly called to her mind her dear friend, Petula who alone had tried to tell her about marriage. That uninitiated girl's starry-eyed imaginings of the rapture to be experienced on the wedding night had prepared her poorly for Alex's animal caresses or for the ultimately rude and embarrassing act of love-making which caused her much agony! Petula had simply not known what she was talking about.

And after all that, there had been last night. Another man, almost a complete stranger, had opened that door just a crack. Petula's innocent chatter now began to make sense..that was the way it should be. Right or wrong or with whomever, she had known a kind of rapture, and she knew finally that she was normal. Her foolish flirting with the Legionnaires was, she saw now, wrong, and she understood Alex's fury.

A great despair filled her. Was she never to know love and have children? Was her lack of arousal the reason for her not having a child? Why couldn't she love Alex with what she had felt last night? Maybe a new land would bring some hope. Thought of a new land cheered her up, and she set to work in earnest.

Late that evening, Alex entertained his own memories of an entirely different sort. Looking over the same garden toward the outreaches of Rome, his thoughts also reached back to Alba. It had been an exciting year for Portia as he introduced her to Roman Society. Not nearly as exciting for him was the final

18

realization that he could never again fight on the battlefield..that and the dubious assignment to duty in Palestine. Nonetheless, it had been a busy year, and he had enjoyed the presence of his wife here with him in this time of transition. Soon, they would leave his beloved Rome.

His gaze swept across the vistas of the city, Rome, and noted the lower areas now filled with mist. He would more than likely end his days away from her, this golden city. He would miss it all..the city, the challenging frontiers, and the excitement of the battles. However, the ache in his bones dulled the luster of the cold mud, the smell of blood..alas, even the smell of parties!

Portia saw him standing there with his arms outstretched on the balustrade. The stance enhanced the width of his back and shoulders. If she were able to forget that he was Alex..if she could think of him as just any man..well, perhaps she could..and she took the fantasy no further. Willing herself to relax, to be open and sensual..yes, to pretend..she half-closed her eyes and drifted languidly toward him. Slipping her right had beneath his left one, she leaned her body against his. Startled, Alex looked down at the golden head on his shoulder/ With his left hand free, he curled it around her and pulled her gently closer.

"Just think. In such a little while, all of this will be a memory. Will you miss it so very much?"

To tell her how much was impossible, utterly. So he lied, just a little.

"No, not so much. Being here would remind me continually that my active days are over. What I am to be will be in another place. Change is always a challenge. I am ready for that change."

"I am glad for you. For us too."

His eyebrows lifted. Had he heard correctly?

"You will miss the parties, though, won't you?"

Closing her eyes to concentrate on her fantasy, she turned toward him, deliberately pressing her breasts against him. Savoring this warmth rising within her, she replied throatily:

"Oh no. I am weary of the chatter, the heavy food and wine. I am sick to death of wine. I have run out of gowns to wear, and I'm getting fat."

Cautiously now, with this unexpected approach, Alex's hand slipped down and gently cupped her bottom which was covered with only the sheerest of chiffon. Feeling her speculatively, he said: "Oh come now, Portia! `Fat'? Why, you feel marvelous to me!"

It was working. It was working..a sensual warmth was rising within her.

"You see? You haven't even noticed that I can wear only these floaty things. Other clothing makes me seem even more plump."

Conversation could continue no longer. Gaius caught up in his own sensuality, let his fingers express a more explicit message as he guided her through the arch into their bedroom.

Her pretense that she was with Partheus held her captive as she stopped in front of the great polished bronze mirror where she oozed from the sensual embrace to pick up her hairbrush and stroke her long blonde hair.

Gaius moved up behind her, and his fingers fondled the supposedly offending curves with feigned evaluation.

"Ah yes. I see what you mean. Perhaps a change of diet will do you good."

Caught up in her own game, unable to resist the humor, she shrieked with laughter,tossed the hairbrush at her pursuer, and ran for refuge beneath the bed covers. What fun!

Alex was right behind her, and the bed was no refuge. Still laughing and terribly excited, Portia found joy in the tussle and the following romp of lovemaking. The wear of the years was gone for Alex in these brief moments of passion, and Portia was swept up in her own ecstasy.

When the moment had passed, and it had been surprisingly brief, Portia sat up and clasped her knees to her chest to look down at the satisfied Gaius. She felt as if the scales had dropped from her eyes now, and she contemplated the familiar lines of her husband's face with a great sense of tenderness. The moment was quite special; the pretense worked. Perhaps it would work again and again, and they could have a good marriage! Maybe the time would come when the pretense would not be necessary.

"Oh, it will be good to have a place that is really home! It will be home in Palestine, won't it, Alex?

"As a matter of fact, it will be. I am told that we will have the one garrison apartment, or, if we decide, we can choose to have a home in the city itself."

Her eyes sparkled..a little girl looking into fairyland.

"How wonderful! A new land, new people, and a new home..living like other people. I have felt so useless, just worrying about which gown to wear to a garden party."

"Yes, I suppose that you have. I hope now that you can be happy as I go about Caesar's Business. "

She sighed, rolled her eyes ceilingward, and fluttered her fingers in mock despair.

"'Caesar's Business'..Legions! I guess..yes. Really, I have been bored with all of this `Caesar's Business' but I suppose that it will go on and on. But maybe..Alex, may I plan a nursery? Oh, Alex, may I?" In the uncertainty of the subject, her voice trilled upward.

No answer. Alex had drawn away unto himself. There it was again, that maddening, impenetrable wall of silence! She looked at him again expectantly.

"May I, Alex?" she repeated.

This time her forcefulness caused him to wince. How could he tell her? Where does one begin? Ultimately, as before, shame and guilt glued his mouth shut.

The frustration of not understanding, of not being able to comprehend this wall of silence so heightened her fury that she withdrew her feet from the warmth of his nearness. Gone was the transient feeling of affection. There was a taint of bitterness in her mouth relating somehow to the expenditure of passion. Nothing she could do or say would breach his silence or even hint as to his aversion to becoming a father.

But she could and she would withhold sex from him. It wouldn't be hard! Perhaps, just perhaps, he would find this marriage as lonely as he had made it for her! Innocent no more, she was strangely ashamed. She knew of her conjugal duties. But until Alex met her at least halfway in marital communication, this part of their marriage would be an impasse. She felt sad. Somehow, she did not like him very much just

21

now. There was only a lingering fondness like one feels for an old friend.

The silence continued with each of them holding fast to a private and personal conviction. The moat between them widened. Gaius felt old, sad, and lonely. How he wished that he could tell her the truth!

"Portia?" he began.

"Yes?" she replied hopefully, thinking that at long last, he would explain his disinterest.

How could he begin..yes, even admit that he was a mere shell of a man and hopelessly sterile? What if she knew that there was no hope for her, that in all of those precious years of her youth she would never be called "Mother"?

"Please go on, Alex."

"Ah..um..oh, nothing."

"That's it..just <u>nothing</u>?"

That's it. Just nothing."

He remained curiously mute. The silence was intolerable. Anything was better than this..if he would only <u>talk</u>!

"Alex, I have been wondering. There was a new name on the guest list which puzzled me, a Centurion Cassius Voltanus. Who is he? Apollus' son died years ago, you told me. Is this Cassius somehow related? Is there a Lady Voltanus?"

And so another game began, one which would become fabric in their lives. This was the "everything is just fine, but leave me alone" game which so many women played.

Alex smiled wryly to himself in the darkness. He understood her purpose in changing the subject and was grateful. Perhaps, just perhaps the mythical gladiator would save his life again!

"Oh, yes, The Mad Greek as you call him."

"Mad Greek? How can Dismas, The Bugler, be Cassius Voltanus? It doesn't make sense!" Her voice trilled in excitement.

Gaius mumbled now, feigning a drowsiness that would protect him from having to explain the whole story.

"Yes, yes. It is he. Go to sleep. We'll talk tomorrow."

"`Go to sleep'?  `Talk tomorrow?' That isn't fair!"

"M-m-m." he replied.

"Oh, Alex, you're impossible!"

Portia flopped down under the covers on the edge of her side of the and curled into a tight little ball. Her eyes were wide with excitement. He did not hear her muttering to herself,

"Impossible is an understatement."

Gaius was really asleep now, but it was only in the early, blue light of a new day that Portia dropped off in sheer exhaustion.

CHAPTER THREE

Rain splashed onto the portico, and there was a chill in the air. Inside, in the room used for entertaining in the Gaius apartment, it was comfortable. A floor brazier glowed brightly and gave off a warmth which spread the perfume from the flower "trees" standing in the corners. There appeared to be sheaves of wild foliage along the walls. Torches, in their brackets on six marble columns which circled the room, sent forth a soft glow filling the whole area. The guests had arrived and were settled on their couches at low tables, chatting and laughing.

The host table had been placed on a small platform, and Portia from this vantage point, was pleased with the room. She had feared that the room would be too small for her plans. However, it was perfect, and the guests were already having fun. Looking toward the far wall, she nodded, and the guests fell silent in anticipation. There was a slight movement in the foliage sheaves as servants, garbed in green, gold, and bronze gowns slipped from between them bearing pitchers of wine. It was a delightful bit of staging which caused the guests to laugh and applaud. The party was off to a good start, and the musicians had plucked at the lyres simultaneously to the appearance of the wine-bearers.

Alex turned to speak with Tribune Librius, his successor at the Praetorium. Portia looked to her left to meet Partheus' eyes. His head nodded to his left as he smiled, and Portia's eyes followed his guidance. Seeing Lady Titus paying devoted attention to her husband, they both laughed discreetly with their private joke.

Partheus turned to his companion, and Portia seized the moment to immediately begin her survey of guests to find Centurion Voltanus. She found no one at the tables who was a stranger to her. Then, her eyes looked toward the entrance. A handsome Centurion standing in the doorway was accepting a goblet of wine from one of the servants. He turned and looked toward Tribune Gaius but found himself looking directly into Portia's violet eyes. Her eyes widened with the feeling of familiarity that came over her. It seemed as though she had always known the man. It unsteadied her, and she felt herself blushing; for he seemed to be no stranger at all! Quite suddenly, she realized that she was staring at him with mouth agape. He gave her a roguish grin unexpectedly and raised his goblet. Without hesitation, she grinned back and raised her own goblet. Together they drank and emptied their goblets with identical movements, like puppets on a string. Slowly they lowered their goblets. Standing there for a short moment, his eyes studied her, dark with intensity. Her eyes misted. Her heart pounded. She dropped her eyes and stared into the empty goblet. She looked quickly at Gaius and saw that he was still in animated conversation with Tribune Librius. Then she glanced at her guests and realized that no one had noticed her caprice. She looked again toward the entrance to find the Centurion with the blue eyes. He was gone! Instantly the party fell flat. Gaius' voice reached her, seemingly from far away. She turned to him with eyes wide, face pale, and hands shaking.

"Are you all right, Portia?"

She nodded with weak affirmation.

Chuckling, Gaius looked into her empty wine goblet and quipped, "I thought you were sick to death of wine!"

It was a reprieve. Portia tittered, then donned the cloak of pretense. A dimpled coquette, she looked up with pixy grin, shook her empty glass, and addressed the world in general:

"But, Alex, it is very good wine!"

Her timing was flawless. Everyone roared with laughter. The storm within her settled now. Gaius continued looking at her.

"Are you sure that you're all right, Portia? You are so pale!"

She played it well, nodding dismally, rubbing her small hands over her stomach, and then shrugging her shoulders in resigned contrition.

"I guess so, Alex. It's the wine, I'm afraid. No matter how good it tastes.."

Her words ended lamely. He finished it for her:

"It was just too much too quickly, right?"

Remembering now how quickly she had downed the wine, and why, her lips twitched in a half-smile. She lowered her eyes so that he could not read her secret and nodded slowly. Almost paternally, Gaius said:

"Well, you eat now..and be careful I'll get some milk for you to drink first." He signaled to a servant.

How very like her father, he was! Annoyance tainted the moment. When the milk arrived, Portia sipped at it tentatively. There was really nothing wrong with her stomach, and she was hungry. While she nibbled with apparent diffidence, Gaius looked on with concern. Then he whispered into her ear:

"If you wish, My Dear, slip out and go to bed. This wine of yours has everyone a bit off balance. They'll never notice that you've gone."

She tried a smile, looking directly into his eyes. Her lips trembled a bit, and she was ashamed.

"I'll be all right now, Alex. Thank you."

The servants began to move the tables and their empty dishes to one side while the guests slid their couches into a semi-circle. The entertainment was to begin. As she exchanged smiles and little waves to her friends around the room, her thoughts raced around in her head. Was that Centurion Cassius Voltanus? Where had he gone? When would she see him again? Did she dare?

The music moved into an exuberant tempo, and the dancing began. Portia leaned into Gaius with her eyes ostensibly focused on the dancers and asked casually,

"Where is that new Centurion, Cassius Voltanus, that you spoke of? Have you seen him? I don't know him, of course."

"Yes, he was here. I noticed him earlier, but he must have left. I don't see him just now."

"Tell me about him. What is all of this intrigue? Last night when I asked, what did you do but go to sleep!"

Alexander's grin was almost boyish as he answered:

"I think I told you that my friend, Apollus Voltanus, was critically ill, didn't I?"

"Yes. Yes, you did. But what has that to do with it?"

"Everything."

"'Everything'? What do you mean by that I am sorry about Legatus Voltanus. He is a wonderful old man, but.."

Gaius studied her intently for a moment. The phrase, "old man", dug in, for he and Voltanus were of the same age! Portia looked at him quizzically, surprised with the acuity of his look and completely innocent of the implication of her words.

Gaius cleared his throat and replied evenly:

"Well, some years ago, Apollus bought a great stretch of land reaching closer to Rome. He still owns it, and the small place where he resides now was built near the end of the property. During this time, he acquired a family of Greek slaves..a man, wife, and a small son. In a short time, a plague swept the country; and both parents died, leaving only the small boy. Voltanus' son also died of the same disease. Dismas was about the same age as Apollus' son, so he became like a second son to my friend."

Gaius paused as if to focus more clearly on the past.

"Well?" Portia queried.

"Are you sure that you wouldn't just prefer to watch the dancers?" Gaius teased.

"Alex!" She spoke in mock petulance.

"Well, time went by. Apollus and the boy, Dismas, became very close. The boy's origin was something that the Legate chose to forget, and so he was trained rigorously for an appointment to the Legion. Actually, Dismas was ineligible, because there was no blood relationship. The best that Apollus could have looked forward to ultimately was that the boy be assigned to the Auxiliary.

Gaius looked down and smiled at Portia's rapt face.

"You see, My Love, your legend has more substance than you had thought."

Portia nodded happily as she replied:

"Yes, I am beginning to see that indeed it does, but where..?"

Gaius interrupted and continued:

"I think, as I look back, that Voltanus was scheming all along to give the boy a decent future."

"Alex, would you be good enough just to stay with the

story?"

"Oh, certainly. Well, Dismas' training was completed, and he had just finished a tour of duty when my bugler was killed. I forgot to mention that along with his military training, the boy studied music with emphasis on trumpet. So, Apollus knowing of my need, wasted no time in having him transferred to my unit as my bugler. Thereafter, at the Battle of The Danube, he made history by saving my life."

"And that's the bugler story you told me about, right?"

"Correct. Almost two months ago, I received Voltanus' letter in which he told of his illness . In it, he also expressed a great concern for the young man and asked me, as if it were a final request, which it might be, that I secure Dismas' future. I wish that I could have seen his face when he got my reply."

"What did you tell him?"

Gaius smiled proudly.

"I told him that I found his boy at the frontier with the Third Legion and had him transferred immediately to my command. By the Imperium of my Office, I conferred upon him full Roman Citizenship. Then, he was eligible, and I promoted him to Centurion, assigned to my staff as my assistant. Best of all, I did what Apollus waited too long to do. I changed his name and gave him a new identity. He became in one wonderful moment, Centurion Cassius Voltanus; and you and I alone will ever know his secret."

Portia was enchanted.

"Go on. Go on! "

"I have assigned Centurion Sinstra to train Cassius, mostly in the matter of what it is to command. The power of Centurion in The Emperor's Army is awesome, but with that is an equal measure of responsibility. The Palestine Campaign, whatever that amounts to, will season him. And unless I am greatly mistaken, our young man will acquit himself in such a manner that Apollus would be proud of his `son'. He will be a noble heir of distinction."

Portia's eyes reflected her great admiration for Alex.

"What a fabulous friend you are, my husband!"

Alex covered his embarrassment with a quip:

"The truth actually is better than your Bugler Story, isn't it?"

They both laughed. Then Gaius went on,

"I have spared you much of the battle-field goings-on. But this is a secret that I have wanted to share with you and you alone, because life can be a bit uncertain in The Military."

Here, he paused and assumed an expression seldom seen by Portia. "You do understand?"

"Oh, yes, I do. But won't someone here in Rome remember that Voltanus's son.."

"Died? No. There will be neither time nor occasion. He's on his way to see Apollus now, as I will be tomorrow. When we return, we'll be sailing for Palestine shortly. This incident will never be a matter of party gossip."

The asperity of his tone when he said "party gossip" was almost a rebuff.

"The secret stops with me."

Applause rippled through the party then as it was beginning to break up. Gaius and Portia stood and waved from their dais; and as he was smiling to the crowd, Gaius said:

"While I'm gone, you'll be in charge of the household. Get us packed and ready to move when I return. Time is short. By the way, your party was a success, but you still look pale."

"I'm going to be better when my head clears up. And I am going right to bed as soon as this is over."

Partheus Sinstra made his way through the departing dancers and took her hand. Gaius' eyebrows wiggled briefly until the Centurion bent low over her hand in courtly gesture and said with some solemnity:

"Your party was delightful, Lady Gaius. They'll talk of this long after you're gone."

"Thank you, Centurion. I am glad to hear you say so."

Both smiled with the party chatter, but Sinstra's mind knew that something had changed. What was the difference in Lady Gaius?

The rain had stopped. Ahead of Cassius, the Appian Way glistened like silver and stretched as an arrow Southward. The cloud cover, as it broke up, allowed shafts of moonlight to beam earthward, almost making candles of the water droplets in the trees. The Bay of Puteoli was about thirty miles away, and it was there on his ranch that Apollus Voltanus lay dying.

Cassius noticed neither the chill nor the beauty of the night. His mind turned in confusion and exhilaration as his great Bay found his own way along the slippery stones. Ahead lay inevitable sadness, but the events behind him shared his attention. Why had the lovely lady behaved as strangely as he? He was delighted, of course, but bewildered. Obviously, she was Lady Gaius. Amazing. Only a few days ago, he was a nobody. then, he was seemingly of importance to his adoptive father. He was also of some moment to the Tribune whose life he had saved, and that only by a twist of fate. Now, incredibly, he was an Officer in the Legion of Rome!

His greatest hope at the moment was to reach his foster father's house in time. The miles stretched ahead, and though he stopped occasionally to stretch, his unaccustomed time in the saddle was tiring and increasingly uncomfortable. Ultimately, he arrived and descended from his weary mount. One of the servants took the reins and led the horse to feed and rest in the stable.

As Cassius mounted the steps of the house, Arius, the senior household servant, took his cloak and helmet and led him toward the increasingly overpowering stench of decaying flesh. Apollus' gaunt body lay in his bed with sheets covering his lower torso; but the upper body exposed resembled wax. The old man's eyes fluttered open, registered his comprehension of Cassius' identity, and he muttered faintly:

"My son."

"Yes, Father."

"You are well?" He smiled slightly with Cassius' obviously robust appearance.

"Yes, My Father. I am well."

"Where is Alex?"

"I know that he'll be coming as quickly as possible. I expect him by tomorrow."

The conversation tired Apollus, and he seemed to drift in and out of consciousness. Then, quite suddenly, his eyes opened and came to sharp focus:

31

"Bear my name well, my son. Hold always before you our motto, `Per omnes ad astra." The first two words were a directive, while the next two stated the objective. "Through all to The Stars!" had been the driving force of his own career, having believed that honesty and determined effort would win over anything.

Then Apollus drifted out again into the nothingness of the unconsciousness. Cassius wondered then..was there a place where gallantry and honor were rewarded forever? He kissed Apollus' waxen hand and placed it back onto his chest. Unaccustomed to tears and embarrassed as he was before the servants, he stumbled through the house and out to the stable, ostensibly to check on his horse. As he leaned against the stable wall, he heard the hooves of another horse and the creak of saddle leather as Tribune Gaius dismounted. Cassius saluted smartly while the Commander tried to straighten up sufficiently to return the salute.

"How is he, Cassius?"

"Alive, Sir, but fading rapidly. He knew me, and I think that when he rouses to see you, it will bolster his strength."

Alex handed the reins of his horse to the stablekeeper and walked rapidly into the house.

The pallor of death lay over Apollus, but he sensed the presence of his visitor. He brightened and smiled. Tears of joy brimmed his eyes, but it was too late for words. His lips formed Alex' name soundlessly. Then he sighed and was gone. The Tribune wept.

CHAPTER FOUR

The rhythmic rumble of oarlocks was unceasing as a hundred oars dipped into the sea. For men manning the ship, the sound was scarcely noticed, but to those unaccustomed to the sea, it was a drumbeat in the brain. The ship's hull creaked as it pitched and wallowed through the waves, and the wind blew incessantly. For the passengers, it was an experience in boredom, uncertainty, and incipient seasickness; but all endeavored to show only stoic unconcern. The nights, however, were a different matter. The roll of the ship, the stench below decks, and the limited space for their occupancy, all combined to destroy peaceful sleep and to erode any sense of well-being.

Cassius and Portia were stripped of the usual social diversions and the possibilities of finding means of being apart. Only her seasickness and the intensity of Cassius' training provided respite; and even then Partheus had to snap his student's attention back from a vague preoccupation with whatever was on his mind. Portia was going through what men have often considered a woman's prerogative, that of being piqued for no apparently good reason. She was miffed because Cassius had destroyed her peace of mind.

Naturally, Cassius picked up her "vibes"and wondered why she seemed to be deliberately avoiding him.

"Isn't that right, Centurion?"

Cassius heard the voice from somewhere and looked up at Partheus in bewilderment.

"Oh, yes. Isn't _what_ right, Partheus?"

"What _is_ right, Pixilated One, is that Rome dominates the world because of her commitment to excellence on the fields of battle."

The teacher laid aside his material and demanded of Cassius:

"All right . What is wrong with you? Are you ill?"

Cassius grabbed his cue quickly.

"Yes, something like that. I haven't been able to sleep. I

can't eat. It must be the sea. "

"<u>Sure</u> it is!" Partheus chuckled. "You act more like a man hopelessly in love! Do I know the lucky maiden?"

Both men laughed heartily, but Cassius was glad that Partheus didn't know that he did know.

Ten tumultuous days at sea ended on a blissfully calm afternoon. Both Centurions were on deck, enjoying a sunset of glorious color. The rays of the setting sun were interspersed through the intensely blue stratus and spread over towering cumulus clouds . The effect was luminescent as if it were staged just for them.

"Isn't it beautiful!" Cassius said.

"Beautiful it is, indeed," Partheus snorted. "But never again, so help me, never again. The sea is not for me!"

"Nor for me either," Cassius replied. "However, duty is duty, and I will go wherever I am sent, though I hope never back to sea. But that reminds me. You made a statement in our lesson this morning that Palestinians hated the Jews. You seemed puzzled as to why."

"Well, not so puzzled as just intensely interested. In truth, `hatred' in this case is split at least three ways. The Jews and Palestinians hate each other, and then both of them hate us too."

"Why is all of that?"

"The Jews and Arabs had a common father, Abraham. Tradition has it that the Jews were `God's Chosen People'..and more of that in a moment. That meant that the Arabs were not. From the old days when the Jews considered themselves to the be `chosen people', anyone else was considered to be Gentiles..in other words, a lesser people. Naturally, that did little for brotherly love. Herod The Great was king over Judea, king over both peoples, and did a good job in keeping the peace. His extensive building programs benefitted Jew and Gentile alike. He allowed the Jews to continue their kind of worship without interference, even to the extent of our being barred from their certain holy places."

"All right. So the hatred between Jew and Gentiles, as you call them, is more or less traditional. But why do they hate us?"

"We are the oppressors in their point of view. We occupy

their land, extract taxes, and to a large extent, control their lives. Their priests also want to control their lives, so they use us as scapegoats to enhance their own importance. Not only that, but there has been of late, a rumor that their God is planning to send them a leader who will restore their independence to them."

"Their `God' as you describe him, must be in disfavor, to say the least, with The Emperor."

"Oh, these things come and go. Meanwhile, we try to ignore as much of this as we can, so long as it does not interfere with the policies of Rome. After all, the Jews were under the control of the Hasmonean Dynasty for a long time, and now they are under Herod Antipas, a son of Herod The Great. We are, in effect, the muscle behind his rule. I believe that our current assignment has something to do with all of this, though I don't know what. "

Partheus finished eating his peach and tossed the seed overboard. Turning to Cassius again, he asked:

"What do you think of all this?"

"Someone wiser than I said that one can learn best when his mouth is closed. So just let me listen."

Sinstra chuckled. "With that attitude, my friend, you will go far."

Their conversation and Cassius' instruction were interrupted with the lookout's announcement that he had sighted land. There was the usual bustle of excitement, the Captain's inquiry as to the bearing of the land sighted, and the passengers all coming topside to share the welcome sight. No one, other than the lookout, could see anything other than still more rolling sea. But how wonderful to consider that, at long last, they could expect to be on dry land again!

The ship changed course slightly in quest of the harbor's entrance, and Portia asked:

"Why are we staying out so far, Alex? The Captain seems just content to be sailing parallel to the shore but still so far out."

Alex pointed with his finger.

"Do you see that line of white water, my dear? The waves are breaking over rocks that you can't see, and the Captain will steer clear of those boulders that could sink us until he finds the channel leading into the harbor."

The time passed with their encountering little other than the few out-bound vessels. Then, they began to see hills, cliffs, and valleys much more closely as the ship's position could be accurately lined up with landmarks ashore. The land seemed to part before them, and they approached the glittering port of Caesarea.

From its inception, it was Herod The Great's bequest to a geographically contradictory land, his own self-edifying monument; and nothing had been spared in its creation.

The crew and passengers stared in awe at the opulence of the port city named in honor of Herod's Patron, Augustus Caesar. The Judean coastline provided no natural harbor, so Herod created one with building a 200-foot-wide breakwater. And on that, 100 vaulted warehouses for cargo were established. Sea-going vessels could sail in and dock, safe from the prevailing currents from the Southwest.

Cassius looked to his left and saw another seawall, this one being semicircular. It was intended to provide a yacht basin whose entrance was flanked by colossal statues. While he continued to stare, Sinstra filled in some additional information:

"You can't see it from the ship, but I have read that Herod imposed a modern grid system in the planning so that, at the intersection of the two main streets, there is a typical Roman forum. And at the Southern end of the North-South roadway, bordered by a colonnaded aqueduct which brings water into the city from springs under Mt. Carmel, there is a magnificent amphitheater."

Cassius was speechless with wonder. Suddenly, the ship came alongside the dock, and lines were tossed ashore to secure the vessel. In a surprisingly short time the docking was completed, and the gangplank was ready for the passengers to disembark. Cassius, Partheus, and two auxiliaries stood smartly at attention as Gaius and Portia walked by and descended the gangplank to go ashore. Gaius was pointing out some points of interest so that he did not see Portia's wandering gaze. She looked into Cassius' eyes for just a moment, long enough to read his expression, and found herself in a daze of enchantment.

"Are you listening, Dear? There are Tribune and Lady Fabius, waving to us!"

". . .Oh, yes. I'm sorry....Oops!"

Her scarf wafted suddenly from her hand, and a capricious breeze rolled it along the wharf toward the ship and the sea. Portia ran in hot pursuit. Then the wind caught it to fling it high into the air where Cassius caught it midflight.

"Oh, thank you, Centurion Voltanus! I might have lost it." She dazzled him with a radiant smile as he smiled somewhat awkwardly:

"You'll never lose it, Lady Gaius, while I'm here."

Both realized that it was a dumb answer, but words really weren't needed for the message between them. She was thrilled, and he felt worse than ever.

The following several days found Cassius and Partheus checking the cargo taken from below decks and directing the crew which had been furnished by Tribune Fabius as they stowed luggage and furniture aboard wagons brought for their transport. The work was demanding, but through it all, Cassius saw a vision of violet eyes, soft red lips, and blonde hair stirred in the wind.

"Oh, Centurion! If the job is done, as I assume that it is, will you dismiss Tribune Fabius' legionnaires so that they can return to their regular duties?"

Damn Sinstra! He was caught daydreaming again, and it angered him.

"They will be dismissed when I have checked the inventory," he replied evenly. Training was one thing; nagging, another. Perhaps it was time that the teacher learned the difference.

Portia and Alexander were welcomed into the off-garrison home of Tribune and Lady Fabius. It was apparent that Fabius had plans for them, but Portia and Gaius were still struggling to overcome the sensations of shipboard life.

"I'm still rocking and rolling to the rhythm of the sea," Portia said.

"Don't worry about it, Little One. You acquired 'sea-legs' as we all did , but this too will pass."

There was a soft, discrete knock at the door.

"The Tribune will welcome your presence, Tribune Gaius, at your earliest convenience." Publius, one of the domestic servants, bowed slightly and hurried away.

"And that translates as 'get with it, my friend'," Gaius growled. With a friendly pat on Portia's beautiful bottom, he slipped out the door and walked across the sumptuously-planted atrium to Fabius'Office.

"Welcome, Dear Alexander! Are you finding your quarters comfortable?"

"More than comfortable, Maximus. They are positively luxurious compared to the cramped quarters of that sea-going tub. We are most grateful for your hospitality."

Fabius' manner was certainly gracious. But there was also about him an air of uneasiness. What was it? Claudia, his wife, seemed serenely happy and probably more than capable to taking care of his manly needs. What, then?

Publius poured a glass of white wine for each of them and left. Making only a brief gesture of best wishes with his glass, Fabius pointed to the chair in front of his desk.

"You'll probably be more comfortable here, Alex. And I forgot to ask you; you do like white wine, don't you?"

Though he despised anything that might challenge his stomach, Gaius smiled his assent and sat down. Then Fabius asked:

"What can you tell us of our situation here, Tribune?"

"Much less than I should like. What can you tell me?"

"We here in Judea are stretched thin. The campaigns on several fronts have served to parade Roman might to our barbaric neighbors, but the only garrison with any demonstrable strength is in Jerusalem."

"Why Jerusalem?"

"Well, there is a turbulence with the Jewish faction, more than usual. Rumors have run rampant for years; but just now, there is talk of the restoration of Israel with a king on the Throne of David."

"What a time for an uprising!"

"At the right time and place, it will have to be put down, of course, which may have something to do with your assignment, though I don't know just what. Meanwhile, we make do here in Caesarea. As you know, this is the principal home of our governor, Pontius Pilate, and he is determined to make a good showing.."

"All of which comes down to a wonderful opportunity for your career, a great place to be stationed, and an awful responsibility to do the impossible with too few to do it. But what do you know of the garrison's strength at Caesarea Philippi?"

"I simply do not know, Alexander. And if this thing with Jerusalem continues to build, much of what is there now may be requisitioned to build up the strength in Jerusalem."

"And meanwhile," Gaius smiled ruefully, "keep ready." Fabius smiled wryly.

"If it were easy, you and I would never be called. Which brings to my mind your own situation. You're eager to get up the mountain to your own command, I suspect. When will you wish to leave?"

"If I were alone, tomorrow at dawn would be my choice. However, Portia has not been well..too much excitement, the rough conditions of travel, that sort of thing. And I'm not at all certain of what her life will be like at Caesarea Philippi. So, despite my own desires..and I know that you understand them perfectly well..I believe a few days here in the glorious city may be time well spent before moving on."

Maximum Fabius smiled appreciatively.

"If your tactics in the field are thought as well as you plan at home, may the gods help the enemy!" Both laughed, and Gaius settled down for an easy visit before assuming the rigors of the task ahead.

But, he wondered, what awaited him in the tangled affairs of Palestine?"

CHAPTER FIVE

Alex dug into the reports on Palestine and discovered some interesting facts. Interesting, yes, but far from helpfully conclusive. Both Pontius Pilate and Herod were politicians, though of a different cloth. Pontius Pilate was eager and active in his obvious desire to ingratiate himself with Rome, while Herod Antipas gave the impression that he was interested in the people. Both, of course, wanted the same thing; only their methods differed. Only a fool would get involved with the politics of the volatile situation, Gaius reasoned.

While her husband was busying himself with what she considered "Caesar's Business" Portia was focused on overcoming the fatigue and seasickness of the voyage. And, of course, she wondered continually as to what was going on with Cassius. Perhaps she should feel guilt, but "should" was way down her list of concerns. Never having felt like this before, she wasn't sure of what she should do. What she did know was that her every waking moment was immersed in the obsession with Cassius.

She was dressing for a day "on the town" when Alex returned to their suite. He was frustrated with the lack of meaningful information on his new assignment and was weary with the effort. But seeing Portia lifted his spirits immediately, and he whistled appreciatively as his eyes feasted on her curves wrapped unadorned in a snug white gown.

"Does Lady Fabius have any idea of the hubbub you're going to cause when you swish into the market place in that outfit?"

"Oh, come now, Alex. You're getting too much rest for my own good." They both laughed a little, but he noted for the first time a sort of smugness..yes, maybe a little boredom in her manner. Well, he could ask anyway.

"Do you suppose that tonight we could..?"

"Please, Alex. Not just yet. You are just too much when you get started."

The comment was flattering, of course, but it was still rejection. There had been too much of that, and he was angered. This delay in getting to his new assignment made him especially antsy, he realized, but he was becoming ever more aware that her mind was somewhere else. She was much too young to be in that vague and senseless condition that older women sometimes got, so what had changed her? Were all young women so unpredictable?

Alex stomped out of the room, but Portia was glad for the chance to think without interruption of Cassius' eyes, his peculiar answer of "you'll never lose it so long as I'm here"?

There was another knock at the door, another interruption from Alex, she suspected.

"Are you ready, Lady Gaius?"

Cute as a pixy in her own right, and obviously ready to impress her guest with Caesarea's opulence, Claudia Fabius stood waiting.

"Ready is an understatement, Lady Fabius. I am eager to see your city."

Both women descended the steps of The Tribune's house and seated themselves in the slave-borne litter. Portia was intrigued with Claudia's throaty laughter and found herself thrilled with the opportunity to see this city built at the dictates of Herod from the ground up.

Sturdy slaves picked up their litter, and the tour began. Claudia was an excellent hostess with an impressive amount of knowledge. She pointed out the gleaming marble facades, the golden cupolas and stained glass windows; she described each as enthusiastically as if it were her own first time to see them. And Pontius Pilate's mansion was utterly breath-taking. They had past this imposing edifice when they started down the colonnaded street leading south to the amphitheater. Magnificent carvings on overhead colonnades preceded the actual entrance; but once inside, Portia was fascinated with the colorful mosaics which lined the walls separating the seating sections. Claudia asked:

"Did you know that before Herod The Great died, he inaugurated the Roman Games for Athletic Competition?"

"No, I did not. Actually, I know very little of the history of this part of the world even though I did grow up near Rome. But then, Rome isn't the whole world, is it?"

"No," Claudia replied, "it isn't the whole world, but it does rule it." Both laughed, and then Claudia asked,

"What did you do in Rome?"

"Well, I went to parties. Then I gave parties. But actually, though you wouldn't know it, I only lived in Rome for about a year. Before I married Alex, I grew up in the cattle country around Alba. When we were married, we lived only a short time in Rome until he was off to the campaigns in Gaul. So, during his absences, I just went back home and picked up my life where I had left it. He was injured pretty badly at the Danube and came home with his awful limp and after that, it was pretty much all party time until we came here. It has been difficult for him, but he's no longer capable of campaign duties in the field. The Palestine Command may well be the means of transition from actual combat, which he loves, to the sedentary duties of command."

Claudia had been taking it all in, though, for some reason, she just wasn't terribly interested in Tribune Gaius.

"By the way," she interrupted, "where is Alba? I haven't heard of it."

"Alba is in the Po Valley, which is West of Rome. My father is a cattleman up there and raises horses too."

"So how in the world did you meet Alexander Gaius that far from Rome?"

"He and my father were boyhood friends. Their families were Equestrians when that title had less to do with wealth than it did with horses. Father chose to remain in Alba and retain his Equestrian title, while Alex preferred the military life and was finally appointed Tribune. You know, I can't remember when Alexander wasn't in my world. I even envisioned him coming to rescue me one day!"

"'Rescue 'you? From what? Your life must have been almost perfect."

"It was, I suppose. Some of my friends in Rome asked that same question..why would I marry Alexander, come to Rome, and leave that wonderfully simple life behind me. But there was the glitter of the city, the excitement of the cosmopolitan life; and I thought, with Alex, all of it would be mine."

"Well, your dreams did come true. But you are so young, and Alexander..oh, he's nice and impressive, but."

"Yes I know. I am so young, and he is old enough to be my father. But back then, I didn't consider age difference as being important. I just didn't know."

Without meaning to do so, Portia seemed suddenly pitiful.

Claudia's eyes sharpened, and she saw her new friend in a very different light. It would be tactless to make further comment on the matter. But she did reach out to take Portia's hand, and Portia silently covered Claudia's. There was intimate understanding, something quite deep and permanent.

"Portia, once you get settled, please come back for a visit. The Games will start in a few weeks, and we two can have such fun!"

"Oh, yes..yes, I will. I am sure that Alex will let me. He will be so busy with `Caesar's Business'.." Portia made a wry face.

For two more wonderful days, the great house by the sea saw little of them They took in every corner of the city. Portia was wide eyed, and Claudia was especially happy to show her all of the best shops. Portia selected silks and brocades for Claudia's gowns and shared with her knowledge of Rome's latest trends in fashion; while Claudia helped Portia in the purchase of drapes, bedspreads, linens, and fabrics suitable for garrison life in a climate greatly different from Rome's. They had a wonderful time, and Portia realized for the first time just how greatly she had missed the pleasure of a close, personal friend.

Now, there was the trip ahead with its adventures. And she wondered, would there be the chance to see more of Cassius? She hadn't forgotten, of course,

CHAPTER SIX

The day of departure for the Gaius Caravan arrived and found Portia and Claudia together beside the garden fountain. Heads close together and speaking softly they said goodbyes as have women the world over with endless words of promise, hugs and eyes filled with tears. Then quickly they walked, hand in hand, the short distance to the garrison gate where the wagons waited.

There were four wagons. the last was filled with Garrison supplies, while the next in line contained their personal household goods from Rome as well as Portia's recent purchases. Transport for servants and their possessions was relegated to the next wagon, while the lead vehicle seemed small and gay by comparison. It was Portia's.

It was equipped with a colorful canopy, and matching silk hung from the canopy frame. For the moment, they were tied back to afford a forward view; but their purpose, when dropped, was to afford her privacy. Leather curtains outside the silk ones were also rolled up. Obviously, they afforded solid protection from bad weather or cold winds.

She giggled as she looked at her wagon, so utterly feminine in contrast to the others. Then, with a final hug and goodbye to Claudia, she climbed into her wagon, dropped casually onto her mattress.. and promptly disappeared from view, shrieking first with surprise then laughter. Then, amid everyone's guffaws, Claudia's scolding voice addressed The Tribune:

"Oh, Alexander, not a feather mattress!"

Portia's golden head and laughing eyes peeked over the edge of the wagon. As it rumbled forward toward the garrison gates, she steadied herself with one hand and waved goodbye with the other until the closing gates hid Claudia from view.

The caravan moved slowly but steadily over the stone-paved road Northward toward Tyre. Occasional sea breezes caressed the travelers, while the wagon teams found the level travel relatively easy. The heavy work lay beyond when they would move up the mountains of the East, across the Jordan Valley, and ultimately Mt. Hermon itself.

The rhythmic rumble of her wagon and its gentle rocking motion made Portia sleepy. She released the rolled up silk curtains, slipped back into her cozy mattress and slept. Eventually, the winter sun was almost directly overhead, and reflections from it flicked back and forth over her eyes until she was suddenly awake again. Where was she, she wondered, until the plodding rumble of the wagon wheels brought her back to the present. Seeing a piece of carpeting atop the boxes up front, she wobbled forward in her feather cocoon until she reached it. When it was plopped over the mattress at the side of the wagon, she found that it afforded a firmer support. Better to ride on top of the feathers than to mush along surrounded by them!

She raised the curtains, inhaled deeply, and was refreshed with the scented sea breezes.

"I hope that Alexander gets duty by the sea sometime," she mused. This was exciting and ever so much cleaner than the smells of Rome.

Looking back toward the West, Portia realized that Caesarea was nowhere in sight, and they were well on their way. The land was wide and rolling toward the sea; and it, in turn, was wide and blue, curving gently over the horizon beyond the shore. Then, as she looked to the East, she saw green terraced foothills, and beyond them, the high forested mountains. Alex had said that they would cross the Mr. Carmel Range and then northward toward Tyre, east of which lay the Lebanon range and the Jordan Valley. Eventually, they would begin their gradual ascent of Mr. Hermon and thence to Caesarea Philippi. When she had asked Alex how long this would take, he replied vaguely something about several days if not a week or so. Strange, she thought. He just never seemed concerned with giving a definite answer to her.

She found it a bit more comfortable to look backward than to look ahead, and so it was that she was suddenly aware of the enchantment of the evening sky. Clouds to the West diffused the sun's rays while those of the Eastern sky caught the nuances of evening..delicate shades of gold, pink, and a misty whiteness which wisped out to the soft blue of falling night.

Having found a level area of suitable size and relatively clear of vegetation, the wagons were pulled into a circle and stopped in preparation for making camp for the night.

"Oh, I must stretch and get onto something solid," she thought. Nothing seemed more important at the moment. Climbing down over the wagon's edge, she discovered that she would have to leap the last few feet onto the ground. She braced herself, took a deep breath, and jumped..right into a pair of strong arms. She looked quickly upward into the face so close to hers, expecting to see Alex, and found Partheus instead.

"Oh, thank you. I guess I didn't care if I took a tumble. I'm fed up with feathers, and I want to feel the good, firm earth again."

He steadied her as she staggered to regain her balance, and they both laughed. Partheus turned then and opened the big box that he had been balancing on his shoulder before catching Portia. Julian came up to help, and as if by magic, a small table appeared complete with all items for a table setting.

"Oh, an outdoor dinner!" Portia chortled.

Partheus' laughter rumbled.

"Well, necessarily so, I suspect. We will have only the basic facilities between here and the garrison, or so we are told. It will be rustic at best, but it will be fun for a while."

"Yes, I am sure that it will be. the air is still warm and pungent with the smells of the country."

Partheus continued with his duties of setting up camp, and Portia walked the length of her wagon to cross to the other side. It seemed impossible that they could have traveled for hours. She searched carefully, but as yet Tyre was nowhere in sight. She breathed deeply and loved the freedom of being out of her wagon. Looking overhead, she saw the first star in the evening sky and wondered whether she would be able to see Cassius.

As she turned to look at the campsite, she realized that she really couldn't identify anyone in the fading light. She was startled to hear her own voice say,

"Where is he?"

She jumped as a deep and familiar voice answered:

"Right here, my dear."

She whirled and blushed with embarrassment. Thank goodness, Alex could not see her red face.

"Oh, Alex. I can't identify anyone in this light. I'm so glad you're here!"

"So am I, Beloved, so am I." He looked up to the on-coming night. "It's getting dark, and there will be no moon. But maybe you and I could enjoy a little walk to stretch a bit. We can't go far before dinner."

"Yes, I should like that. It will help me to get my balance again. But, Alex, we must fix my wagon!"

There it was, that odd thing of her thinking of two completely different things at the same time. She so reminded him of a child. Her concerned sincerity about a such a small thing amused him, and they both laughed.

"Oh, I'm sure that something can be done about it. But can you sleep on it tonight?"

"Of course I can. The feathers are great for sleeping. But for sitting? No way!"

They were still chuckling as they walked back into camp and sat to eat. The campfires were glowing, and the luscious fragrance of baking bread and sizzling meat filled the air. The traveling all day in the open air and the smells of evening grew eager appetites, and there was little time wasted on talk. Portia did see Cassius in the distant glow of the fires as the meal was finishing. Only a brief lingering glance was their solace.

The fires were banked, and the food was put away. Portia climbed into her featherbed, settled down restlessly, and dreamed of a tomorrow.

The following morning found them underway shortly after dawn. As their road wound past Tyre. Portia could hear some dogs bark, and the penetrating call of children's voices, but the town was too far away to see or hear more. However, it was enough to confirm their location as Alex had told her. Soon they would climb over the range of mountains ahead and drop down into the Jordan Valley. Confirming her thoughts, the wagons turned toward the rising sun.

Ahead lay Mt. Lebanon and the Jordan Valley. Alex had not yet built the solid seat that he had promised, so Portia hopped down and walked beside her wagon. The caravan continued upward past the terraced gardens with their ripening produce into a terrain of yellow sand and rocks. Well-worn footpaths criss-crossed the hills, and Portia was fascinated by the sturdy, dark-complexioned people peering at the caravan from beneath burnooses and heavy travel cloaks. The children were as children everywhere, scampering and noisy. The big eyes widened and stared in curiosity, their faces beautiful in the innocent wonderment of seeing something new and different. Roman soldiers and travelers in colorless garb were nothing out of the ordinary; but wagons trailing each other in caravan were a novelty indeed.

Then she became aware of a strangeness in the passers-by. They seemed to lift their cloaks in front of their faces as if to shield them from dust. But there was no dust, only an unmistakable glint of hatred in those dark eyes. There a child jumped out to one side and stuck out his tongue in derision; his childish voice strident with some sort of garbled insult before he was grabbed back into the group by an adult.

Then, as her wagon topped a rocky hilltop and started the descent, Portia caught her breath and immediately forgot the foot travelers. They were starting down into the Jordan Valley. Nothing she had heard of its beauty had prepared her for the vision she beheld....its green, lush beauty spreading beside the winding Jordan river was a sight to behold. Looking down the road into the Valley the verdure increased; but as the river traveled south and the valley widened to include Lake Huleh, the expanse of cultivated fields in shades of green was breathtaking. The road they traveled meandered north and south as it moved down the rugged hillside. To Portia the road appeared to be a thread twisting and turning between the foothills and the lake. In the distance southward. there appeared to be a larger body of water though all she could see was the blue of the Jordan flowing toward it, but even here near Huleh the lush vibrancy of growth beckoned. The road was turning north along the floor of the valley toward another mountain range lying directly in their path. Towering over steep ridges and the flow of foothills at the base, was the snow-capped beauty of Mt. Hermon.

"That must be Mt. Hermon." she muttered and then smiled in delight. "That bit of white I see up ahead on the slopes must be Caesarea Philippi!"

Meanwhile, everyone riding in the wagons had jumped down to move among the trees and pick fruit. They ate as they walked but also filled every available space in the wagons with their plunder. Portia had never tasted figs as large and sweet. What they took appeared to be growing wild, for there was no evidence of people or farms such as seen in the greenbelt to the south from the high road of their travel.

It was late afternoon as they finally started up the slopes they had seen ahead. It was later yet when the weary, dusty group looked up to see the mountain city with the Garrison at its feet. It wasn't that it was so far up as much as that they had been on the road since dawn. It was amazing what energy that sight put into their travel.

Looking up toward that which promised food and bath, Portia wondered where Alex could be. As if reading her mind, - he called out from the other side of her wagon.

"Well, Portia -- there is home!"

She smiled at him and her voice was filled with excitement...

"I am going to like it here...I think..it is so different. A bit wild and mysterious!"

The wagons moved out once more and it seemed that this time even the horses moved eagerly!

Cassius astride his horse at the front of the caravan, found his gaze settling on the golden head in the first little wagon moving toward him. She looked up. Their eyes met. He was stirred as though they had touched. She smiled ever so faintly and he could believe he saw the flicker of something like fear shadowing her eyes. The wagon moved on, leaving Cassius with eyes staring into space and a frown creasing his forehead.

It was at this moment that Sinstra rode up beside Cassius, noticed the frown and asked:

"What is troubling you, Voltanus?"

Cassius snapped to attention with a reply,

"Oh...greetings, Sinstra...why, these people we passed back there. Were they Jews or Arabs? You have helped me understand the 'why' of the look of hatred of the Jews for us...now I don't know the difference between the Arab and Jew.....they all seem to dress alike?"

Sinstra laughed,

"That isn't too hard to explain. But, I'll go into it quickly when we get settled in .. up there.." He gestured toward the Garrison. "It'll be easier with a hand drawn illustration. Right now it isn't that important and we must get where we are going before too much light is gone."

"Right you are. I am just too curious for my own good......up we go!"

He spurred his horse on to the head of the column with Sinstra right on his heels.

Arrival at the Garrison was without much fanfare. The gates swung open and the caravan rolled through. A Legionnaire with a few Auxiliaries greeted them, directed them to their respective quarters and immediately set about unloading the wagons.

Portia was thrilled with the adventure of a new home and determinedly dashed about in a quick tour of their elegantly furnished quarters. However, with Auxiliaries all over the place moving in their belongings, she knew she would have to wait for the dreamed of bath and slipped downstairs and out through the kitchen to the tree-studded courtyard. Following one of the Auxiliaries directions she finally found the gate to the Garden. It was delightfully located, as far as she was concerned, being set apart in back of the their own quarters and between that building and the outside wall of the Garrison itself. It was not in a handy "drop in" location but, rather, so situated that anyone entering through that garden gate had a rightful purpose in entering -- either to garden or to rest.

Opening the gate and entering, Portia felt an instant peace. There was an order here in that the small orchard was in one place, flowers in another and the vegetables in another with paths bordering each. But that was where the order stopped. Lush growing took over and there was a delightfully wild atmosphere. What a sanctuary!

Looking over the wall to the East she could believe she was home in Alba with the mountains and the pines!

The orchard was thick with tree branches interlocking.

As she tiptoed under the trees, even while she wondered at her own caution, she reached the far corner where the Garrison walls met. There a tree had squeezed its branches against both walls so that they curved downward and formed a tiny, shadowed room. How cozy! She dropped to the ground, leaned against the tree and peeked through the branches and watched the moving shadows as the wind stirred the trees. So quiet! Suddenly she realized how tired she was. Stretching luxuriously and standing up to make her way back to her new home she thought how wonderful it would be to sleep in a real bed again. Giggling she remembered her initiation to the wagon's featherbed.

Entering she found Lea and Alex in a flurry of activity sorting his personals from the household items, neatly stacked but in no order of relativity, in the middle of the great room's floor. How like men! She took herself aback, for she did respect soldiers....after all they didn't know which crate or barrel held what!

With a laugh she also set to work. She, after all, had packed their personal items and knew which held what!

"You are in such a hurry, Alex. Your orders must have been urgent?"

"'Immediately' has been altered by my interpretation of that to 'as soon as possible' -- after all it takes a bit of doing"

"Well, at least you are still in the travel mood."

They all laughed and with the three of them working they shortly had all of Alex's clothing and personal items repacked.

Portia climbed into the big bed with a sigh and flopped down completely relaxed..but before she reached the haven of sleep Alex joined her -- wearing a big smile and little else. With him leaving next day for Jerusalem his words shut the door on any evasion of the matter at hand.

"You know I haven't invaded your privacy, so to speak, well--since before we sailed from Rome. Loving you..wanting you..knowing how I'm going to miss you when I am so very far off in Jerusalem....may I..??"

Portia smiled up at him, unable to resist his pleading tone. He moved close to her and leaned down to kiss her lips. His hands were gentle and she could do nothing other than wrap her arms around him.

Alex drowned himself in the wonder of her. If any thought crossed his mind at all, it was with gratitude for her welcome and the fact that he, for once, was able to show his love and endeavor to make her happy. Mostly, though, he was swept up in his own passion and fulfillment as he had not been for many months.

Alex slept deeply, dreamlessly while Portia listened to his steady breathing. Wiping away tears she felt a sense of infidelity -- not to anyone so much as to herself. This intimacy had told her, finally, that not even considering the unbidden attraction to the new Centurion - she did not love Alex. Surely not as a woman should love her husband..that emotion had always been missing between her and Alex. The fact of such emotions existing had been revealed in the bewildering jolt of her encounter with Partheus Sinstra. Then had come the sudden emotional impact of just the sight of Cassius Voltanus....just looking at that man had aroused within her feelings she had no idea she possessed.

Staring up into the canopy overhead, the parade of her party-girl life skipped before her eyes. She shuddered in distaste and realized, quite suddenly, that she was growing up! Why had it taken so long? Before falling to sleep came the realization that she could be fearful of the future...how would she cope?

Late the following morning, with her eyes still closed, she awakened to the knowledge that Lea stood by her bed and that Alex was gone from the room.

Opening her eyes slowly and then blinking against the bright light, she turned her head and looked up at Lea.

"What time of day, Lea? The room is so bright!"

"Almost time for the mid-day meal, Lady Gaius. The Master insisted you not be aroused before now, but I know you would like to bathe and dress before lunch."

"Oh, my yes! He leaves right after lunch! Whatever

possessed me, do you suppose?"

"Well, you put in a full day even after half a day of travel -- and, as you know, we did a lot of unpacking and repacking and.well, perhaps you got to bed late..."

Lea smiled knowingly, for not often were servants dismissed from quarters by the Tribune.

Portia grinned, remembering the end of the day.

"You're right, you know...a very full day!"

"Your bath is ready, M'Lady."

Lunch was a pleasant affair with Portia her usual, bubbly self asking a thousand questions about what he would be doing and when he would return..and he hadn't even left yet! Alex grinned as he tried to answer only to be interrupted with another question.

"Portia, would that I was as wise as you are inquisitive! I don't know the answers. I only know that we leave today as soon as possible. I am leaving Voltanus here for a month or so, to do all the necessary, pesky record-work. You will be advised as to whether you are to be in Jerusalem or here. From what little I do know, I suspect you will remain here and visit Jerusalem. We'll have to wait for developments."

Portia's head was in a sudden whirl. Voltanus would be here! She had just assumed he would be going with Gaius. Her voice was tremulous as she said...

"Oh, how wonderful....to see Jerusalem..if for only just a visit!"

Alex stood up and took her hand lifting her to her feet and into his arms. He gave her a great bear hug and a long kiss. It was goodbye and he would miss her.

Remembering last night made leaving more endurable.

"Goodbye, Portia dear...take care of you. No need for you to come down to the Assembly area. We are going to make short work of this leave-taking. It is a long trip. Just do your waving from the balcony."

"Goodbye, Alex. Take care. I will be anxious to hear from you.if there is time for a letter."

"I will be in touch -- never fear."

With that he was gone. Portia, at her post on the balcony,

watched the departure of the tiny group and waved. The gates closed behind them.

CHAPTER SEVEN

Cassius had been standing just outside the office door watching the departure. He turned to reenter and, in so doing, looked up toward the Gaius` balcony seeing Portia standing there looking down at him. His heart leaped within his chest. Quickly he bowed to her and took a deep breath as he straightened and looked up at her. She grinned and waved to him. He smiled back and he could feel his face flush in spite of himself. Quickly he stepped back into the office. However, all thought of work or duty had left him and he was experiencing a sense of tremendous excitement.

He stood inside the window and looked eagerly toward the Gaius apartment, captured in a totally irrational sense of rapture. How long he stood so he didn't know, but it was a bit of time. So it was that he saw Portia, dressed in entirely different garb, suddenly appear on the top of the stairs leading to the apartment. Her long and full tunic clung to her body in the breeze as she descended the stairs very quickly. She moved rapidly across the courtyard toward the office. Cassius let out his breath which he had been holding since first seeing her on the stairs and his heart was pounding inside his chest. Suddenly, very close to the office now, Portia slowed and with a casual, measured step moved toward the door. In spite of his own erratic emotions, Cassius realized she was in an identical emotional state. When she cautiously bent forward to peek inside, he had turned to face her and she found herself staring at his chest. Standing up straight, she was staring right into his eyes. She burst into embarrassed laughter. Joining her outside the door he was also laughing. They were both feeling unrealistically exuberant. Thinking frantically of something to say to cover this vibrating moment, Portia spluttered:"Centurion Voltanus, guess what. I have found the Garrison Garden...it is lovely. Do you have time for me to show you?"

"Why not? I feel like taking the afternoon off anyway. It has been a frantic arrival and 'sending off' period. I certainly am a bit tired. Let`s do it."

"Good...come."

She turned and led the way to the pathway ending at the gate in the wall joining the apartment section to the outside garrison wall. She stopped in front of the gate and whirled to face him, not realizing how close to her he was. He reached out to grasp the top of the gate to steady himself in the sudden stop, and found himself against her with her sweet breath against his neck. She tilted her head to look up at him. Their closeness was spellbinding. Her mouth opened in a soft gasp and she flushed. He looked directly into her violet eyes and his emotions had him trembling. Slowly his hands moved down from the top of the gate to close gently on her shoulders. They were trembling. He ever so easily turned her to face the gate and her hand opened the latch. In one movement they stepped inside and the gate shut behind them. She was helplessly captive in overwhelming emotions, unwilling to fight against it.

She stood very, very still and his fingertips began to tighten on her shoulders. She turned in his grasp with a tiny, guttural cry. As he caught her to him their lips met. For a few moments they were bound together, their lips crushing, seeking.

Cassius fought for sanity and his hands grasped her shoulders to move her away just a little and his lips moved. Barely audible, he spoke haltingly.

"I am sorry...forgive me, Lady Gaius."

"No...nothing to forgive, Centurion Voltanus...I ..I stopped too..too suddenly and - - " her eyes were looking at his lips. Very slowly they opened wide as her head tilted back ever so slightly. They gazed at each other breathlessly.She continued in a whisper,

"....it doesn't really matter...I..have - oh, please -please hold me!"

His arms moved swiftly to clasp her to him and their lips met in a long, hungry kiss. Her arms found their way around his neck. Finally, breathing deeply, they pulled their heads back and gazed at each other in wonder.

"Lady Gaius...this, this shouldn't be..." he whispered.

"I know. I know..but..Well, I have hoped...thought it would be for so long.." she whispered back as she pulled his head down again and their lips met once more.

His hands took on a life of their own and began to caress her waist.her hips, pressing her closer. Her head dropped back and his lips avidly kissed her throat, her neck. Her soft moan as she sagged against him caused him to lift his flushed face to hers and one of his hands reached up to push her head toward him.

Her lips moved in a whisper.

"You are right...it should`t be...but it is...it will be must be.I - I can't be without you - - now."

Tears crept from her eyes and he kissed them away, aware that tears in his own blurred his vision. He reached up to wipe them away. Straightening, she stepped back from him, ever so slightly, and whispered

"I must go in and try to get my head straight. And,Cassius...please, meet me here after supper tonight?"

Aware of her use of his first name, he smiled as he raised a finger to gently touch her chin.

"Yes, my darling Portia."

"Ohhh...she murmured softly. "...thank you."

In slow motion she lowered her head, not daring to look at him, turned and drifted back through the gate. Holding the gate to keep it from clicking shut, Cassius closed his eyes, muttering brokenly,

"Oh, what am I to do...I love her so..."

As in a dream, Portia made her way along the proper path and then up the stairs to the Gaius apartment. Once inside she leaned weakly against the closed door with her eyes closed and tears trickling down her cheeks. Absently, her hands lifted to wipe away the wet as she muttered to herself,

"What am I to do? I love him...that I know. But even in spite of Alex, I love him. I haven't the courage to walk away ....no - no let it be...I want him, I need him..."

Deliberately opening her spirit to the ecstasy she had just experienced, Portia let herself go. As the waves of love and desire swept through her again, she moaned in joy and threw herself onto the bed and rolled back and forth. Burying her face into her pillow, she fell into her private world of joy...and slept.

Almost an hour later Lea knocked on the door. Getting no response, she entered carrying clean laundry to be put away. She stopped quickly, seeing the sleeping form and tiptoed to the bedside. Portia slowly awakening, became aware of her presence and rolled over onto her back smiling broadly inwardly filled with joy.

"I'm awake! I had the most luscious nap!"

"Good. I think we all need a day or so of doing just that!"

"Lea, I'm a bit lost in time right now...how far away is supper?"

"Oh, let me think..." she paused as she put the linens away in a cupboard. "...ah, seems that Petta was just now trying to figure out something for an early supper today. Is that all right with you?"

"Wonderful. I'm starved. You know what....I would like an early bath so that after an early supper, I can do more of this sleeping thing!"

Lea burst into laughter.

"Smart girl...out to please everyone, you are! We were all hoping for an early to bed night. I'll tell Petta...and then I'll be right back to fix your bath."

Portia grinned to herself and went into her clothing alcove to finger through her cloaks and tunics. She chose a soft woolen cloak lined with satin and then found a very special tunic. It was short and made of chiffon with lace trim and the soft pink blended so well with her skin she giggled. She heard Lea at the door and quickly snatched her bath cloak and came out of the alcove as Lea started to fill the tub.

It was fun to watch the tub filling routine. The old fort's plumbing here was clever. Lea turned the huge marble handle to start a steady parade of small wooden buckets, filled with hot water, move up into the bath through a special opening in the floor. They were fastened to a special chain in such a way as to move up to a height a bit over the top of the tub and then travel about a foot at which point the chain made a sharp downward turn tipping the buckets to empty the water into the tub and then begin their downward journey to the kitchen.

Watching, Portia giggled. Lea turned her head with a smile and looked at her Mistress. Standing up she motioned Portia to come to the tub and the handle as she spoke, "Come....you can turn them off when there is enough water. It is fun to watch...but I do it so often and I can go down and help Petta get the supper ready."

"Thanks, Lea...it is such fun to watch. I hope I have sense enough to turn the handle." Portion chortled to herself with each bucket dump. Finally, there was enough water and she slid into the tub which was so full of water the bubble beads were at the very edge of the tub and Portia did look swamped.

Day dreaming of the coming evening she finally climbed from the tub and bothered not at all with dressing but just wrapped the bath cloak around herself and curled up on the couch to await the supper tray.

It was not long before Lea returned with the dinner tray, turned back the bed covers and left with Portia's"thank you" following her as she left the room.

"I will be back for the dinner tray in a little while, Lady Gaius." she called back.

Finishing her food, Portia curled up on the couch and continued her wondering about the coming evening. Lea believed her to be sleeping when she came back for the dinner tray and was startled to hear Portia speak.

"Goodnight, Lea. Get a good night's sleep."

"Oh...thank you..yes..I will, and you too."

Alone, Portia stretched and grinned to herself with her delicious secret and snuggled down to wait for dark to descend.

She fell asleep. With a start she awoke to find it dark. How long had she slept!! Jumping to her feet, she hurried into the chosen tunic and then swiftly brushed her hair until it was its softest. Then, slipping into the woolen cloak and covering her head with the hood, she stepped out onto the stairs and stood listening intently for a moment or two. There were no sounds of activity anywhere. Tiptoeing to the bottom of the stairs she moved with soft, floating motion to the corner of the building and the garden gate.

She turned and looked everywhere for sight of movement.

Finally, opening the gate she slipped inside and gently closed it behind her. The latch made no sound. Finding the bench she sat down to wait.She turned when she heard a scuffing sound at the outer wall, and saw a form drop to the ground inside and stand very still. Watching, she knew by the walk it was Cassius. Quickly she stood and held out her arms.

Swiftly he clasped her to him, whispering,

"I am sightseeing in the city -- in case you wonder where I am." his chuckled rumbled in her ear.

"--and I am fast asleep...according to Lea!"

She giggled softly, then whispered...

"Come. I have found a special place." She took his hand and led him into the Orchard and to the far corner where the garrison wall turned. Here with the tree crushed against each of the walls to form an enclosed bower, it was like night itself but without the glow of even the moon. As she turned toward him she shed her cloak and handed it to him.

"Spread this on the ground so we will have a softer, smoother place to sit."

He did as she suggested and turned to her with a smile she did not see.

"Did you say `sit'?"

" Yes...why?"

"All right. Sit here beside me."

As she sat down, his hands reached up to help her and slipped unexpectedly under her tunic which he could not see in the dark.. The effect was electrifying to them, wiping away all restraint between them. With his mouth on hers he clasped her to him and they stretched full length on the cloak. His hands on her body built a fire within her. Nothing mattered but his touch. He had shed his tunic also. Her hands pulled him close...closer. With their bodies pressed together, the world ceased to exist. Their lips pressed together seemed to seal a promise. Cassius gently caressed her body as their lips clung. He whispered her name, even as he claimed her. A tiny cry escaped her lips in that moment of consummation . Their love shut out the world.

The chill of the night forced reason upon them, and they rose to their feet. Cassius slipped into his tunic and cloak and turned to Portia who had folded her cloak and put it in the corner of the walls behind a tree branch. She had on her tunic and for the first time he saw its sheerness as a shaft of moonlight beamed through the tree's branches.

"Are you going to leave the cloak here?"

"Of course."

"But..you'll freeze..."

"No...I'm going to run too fast!"

She moved in very close to him and looked up, pulled his head down and whispered in his ear..

"We need it here! While everyone else sleeps!!"

He grabbed her to him in a fierce hug and kiss and with his lips against hers, "Oh, how I love you -- love you. When shall we meet again...like tonight?"

"Tomorrow night, the night after, and the night after..."

"Oh...Portia!"

And so they parted that first night and the many nights that followed. Days and nights rolled into three weeks, four.

Nothing would change. They were so in love. However, no such course is ever smooth..never has been.

At the end of the fourth week, Portia came to the inevitable conclusion that she was terribly tired...even sick tired! Goodness, this morning she had quite unexpectedly lost her breakfast and the very thought of food repelled her. What could be making her so tired? All she had done week in and week out was day-dream through the days waiting for the night time. But, oh...the night times! She smiled ecstatically remembering the night time. And, then, of course she had slept soundly clear into the mid-day, every day. All this mind-searching was taking place as she stood in front of her full length dressing mirror naked and brushing her hair. Her eyes idly studied her body. She frowned. Was she getting thinner? Very! Well, perhaps she had better start 'eating what was put before her' as her father used to say...despite her lack of appetite! All she really wanted was to be loved by that wonderful, delicious man! Her leg and back muscles did ache! She giggled to herself...immediately deciding to take a hot bath and a long nap. That might help.

But, of course, nothing did. The sick spells continued.

Strangely, it was always in the morning -- that is for the most part. Another annoyance made itself known. Her breasts hurt...the nipples most of all. It was difficult but she kept all of this to herself. Cassius never had a clue.

He did know something was afoot, however. There was a sense of quietness about his Portia..a lack of her usual `bounce '. She seemed preoccupied. But he dismissed it to fatigue. Both of them had been overdoing the night time activities. Even he himself, was tired! Fortunately, he had gotten everything up to date and records packed for transport to Jerusalem. Now, he was just waiting for order from Jerusalem and he could relax a bit.

It was two weeks later that the Jerusalem Courier did arrive at the Philippi Garrison. He had an official communication for Centurion Voltanus and a letter for Lady Gaius.

CHAPTER EIGHT

Alexander Gaius stood before the arched window of the quarters assigned to him in the Antonia Praetorium,. He felt the cold uneasiness so familiar to him, that peculiar building up within himself of the courage necessary to face another day of battle. His battles had until just recently been just that, with men and horses fighting and screaming in orgies of blood. But this was different. And without his really knowing why, this seemed all the more formidable. Pontius Pilate would not have summoned him, a relatively obscure Tribune of the Roman Army, unless there was an unusual need. In the light of cold logic, such political "unknown" and their men were expendable without causing potential embarrassment to the likes of Pilate. What could Pilate want? Well, he would find out soon. He and Centurion Sinstra had just received a polite summons; they had been invited to dine with Tiberius' Lieutenant himself, the procurator of all Judea, Samaria, and Idumea.

Sinstra knocked politely at his door, and Gaius called out:

"Come in."

The Centurion entered and snapped a crisp salute to Gaius who returned it and smiled:

"I see that you're ready."

"Yes, Sir, I am. I hope that he food is plentiful."

Without further small talk, Tribune Gaius put on his helmet, and two of them marched with as much elan as Gaius' arthritic hip would allow along the corridor, down the flight of stairs, and up stairs again at the end of the courtyard of Pilate's elegant palace which was his residence when he was in Jerusalem.

The Commander had long been accustomed to the pomp and glory of military trappings, but the Palace surpassed it all. In the glow of late evening and the flicker of torchlights, the light-colored stone of which the Palace was built glowed with the unique warm radiance characteristic of Jerusalem. As if reading Sinstra's thoughts, Gaius said:

"You know, it is truly remarkable. It looks like this in either sunlight or moonlight. I wish Lady Gaius could see it."

The guards at the entrance saluted and swung wide the great doors. Partheus stepped aside for Gaius to enter and surreptitiously ran his hand over the stone of the wide, glowing archway. He smiled to himself; it wasn't that different. It was still just stone.

They were shown into the Library where Pilate awaited them. He moved from behind a long table which was loaded with scrolls and greeted them with warm cordiality.

"I am so glad to see you, Tribune Gaius and Centurion. Your reputation has long preceded your arrival, and I can see now why the Emperor spoke of you so highly."

Gaius chose to remain silent for the moment, and Pilate continued:

"We have a situation which can best be described as delicate, and I have wanted to get your analysis without the hungry ears of servants to hear it. We will serve ourselves in our simple meal without attendants. Don't you agree?"~

"Certainly, Governor. But I think we'll probably do more listening than offering our counsel."

They had been following Pilate down a polished corridor to the Dining Room, but they realized that they could have found it easily simply by following their noses. Platters of steaming beef, quail, and chicken awaited them on a round triclinium with three encircling couches. Goblets of wine, of course, marked each place.

The three men chose their food and settled down on the couches next to the triclinium. Picking up a piece of quail and licking away the extra sauce over the meat, Pilate asked:

"What have you thought your mission to be, Alexander?"

Surprised with the intimacy and with the question, Gaius replied:

"Well, I had assumed of course, that you have wished me to take over the Garrison."

"Good..good!" Pilate munched thoughtfully on his meat before continuing.

"That is good, because there is no chance at all that anyone will suspect."

"'Suspect'? What is there to suspect?~

"You know, of course, that the Garrison is under the command of a worthy and capable Tribune. But that's not the point, except that I have no intention whatsoever of replacing him. He is adequate, though I am not certain of his loyalties. Herod's reach may even touch my own people. That is why you are so valuable."

Gaius was stunned. The troops of the garrison at Caesarea Philippi had already been transferred to Jerusalem and, in fact, were a sizable part of the force at the Praetorium. Of what possible use could he be if, as a commander, he had no troops to command? Best to remain silent.

"So you're wondering, Valiant Warrior, if not to command..what?"

"Correct."

"You have rendered great services to Rome. You have fought bravely and wisely. Your tactics at the Danube were brilliant. And that is why you are here. Nothing you have ever done will compare with your services now."

Gaius knew the tactic well. Build up the ego, then let the simpleton sacrifice himself for the objective.

"In a word," Pilate continued, "I need your counsel. What do you know of Jesus?"

"Only what I have heard. Principally he seems to have excited the Jews with what I have heard to be remarkable feats of healing. Is he dangerous to your program?"

"'Program'? I have no program. I wish that I did. Right now, I'm just riding out the storm. But to answer your question, he is not directly dangerous to us, but he could embarrass us greatly."

Partheus felt greatly ill at ease and concentrated on eating and drinking the excellent wine. But Pilate watched him carefully.

"Our wine is delicious, is it not, Centurion? And, by all means, enjoy, enjoy!"

The condescension was not lost on the junior officer, but play it straight.

"Thank you, Sir. I really was quite hungry."

Pilate smiled, then turned his attention back to Gaius.

"Let me put it on the line for you, Tribune. I have pitifully few soldiers available to me in Jerusalem. If this Jesus should choose to lead an uprising as thousands think that he will, I simply haven't the power to stop him. My career could be over, and The Emperor could face a catastrophe here because of my failure. What would you do?"

The Tribune was silent in thought.

"Only we know of your problem; and, at that, you may not have a problem. Why not use the time we have to explore the enemy?"

Sophisticate that he was, Pilate asked:

"How?"

"Have you any dependable information to date that Jesus does plan an uprising?"

"No, nothing specific that Jesus himself plans to overthrow our government, though I have read of a prophecy that the Jews themselves seem to believe. About six hundred years ago, one of their prophets..a fellow called Daniel..predicted the rise and fall of several empires, and his prophecies to date have all come true. All of that may or may not have any bearing on the present.

Gaius himself had never concerned himself with such fantasy; but, seeing that Pilate might seriously consider it, cautiously ventured:

"Why not let me slip a man into his camp, Governor? With so many people coming and going, he'll never suspect. I have a fellow in my command who might easily be thought to be Jewish. We could slip him in, let him look and listen, and find out first hand what this rabbi is up to. What do you think?"

"Perhaps, perhaps. But if he is found out, I can have nothing to do with it."

Gaius noticed with quiet amusement that Pilate unconsciously turned one hand within the other, as if unconsciously washing it.

"It has seemed to me that the Jews are controlled pretty largely by their priests. Their Sanhedrin appears to make policy, and they follow. How does Jesus stand with them?"

Pilate chuckled.

"They appear to hate him, and his scathing attacks on the two major factions, the Pharisees and the Sadducees, have not endeared him. Furthermore, his so-called miracles among the masses, healing lepers, giving sight to the blind and the like..these have given him tremendous power and undermined the leaders. He's definitely not their darling."

Gaius gazed pensively down into the depths of his glass.

"Perhaps you have only to wait and do nothing. If Jesus should move to rebellion, the Sanhedrin can't afford to join him; because that would only further their own loss of command. On the other hand, if he continues as he is..healing the sick and performing other miracles, who has need of the priests? Either way, the fight is Jew against Jew, while we stay out of it. Governor, do you really believe that you have a problem?

Pilate's expression did not change except for his eyes which opened wide with comprehension. Then he permitted himself a discreet chuckle:

"By the gods, Tribune, I think you're right! For them the enemy is within." He sighed as if greatly relieved.

"Eat..eat and enjoy! And Zeus help the enemy!"

Gaius knew that he had been had, that a politician had picked his brain, and he had nothing to show for it. He asked:

"And what of us, Sir? Am I to return to Caesarea Philippi, even though I have no troops ? What of my command?"

"All in good time, Alexander, all in good time. Meanwhile, I want you here. I may need you. Your career is in my hands, and you will be taken care of."

"And what shall I do here, Procurator?"

"You and the Centurion here will be my honored guests. There will be parties and speeches of praise for your gallant career! And I want Herod to wonder what I'm up to. Also, it will be well for the present garrison commander to give serious thought to his own career..you know, think out just where his loyalties should lie. No, Alexander, you will remain while they shake in their boots!"

"And what of the idea of planting a spy within the Jesus camp?"

"Excellent! I will want his report not later than the Jewish Passover in April."

The following morning found Gaius up early as was his habit. He had observed long ago the corrupting power of the easy life; but, if he forgot, his irascible stomach would remind him. Bathed and shaven, he had eaten simply and settled down to dictate orders for Cassius' new role. He enjoyed having the bright young Greek slave assigned to his staff to do nothing but take care of his correspondence. Leaning back now comfortably in his comfortable chair, he began:

"To: Cassius Voltanus, Centurion,
             Emperor's Garrison at Caesarea Philippi.
From: Alexander Gaius,
             Tribune, Staff of Pontius Pilate,
             Governor of Judea, Samaria, and Idumea
Subject: Assignment to Temporary Duty

You will detach yourself from all duties at Caesarea Philippi upon receipt of these orders. Securing such supplies as you may need for extended duty in the field, including support animals. You will proceed to an appropriate locale, possibly Capernaum, and locate the rabbi known as Jesus of Nazareth. In the guise and manner of a local Jew, you will find, infiltrate, and follow this Jesus, making note of any indication of his organizing an army or speaking seditiously against the Emperor.

You will compose your report and present it to me in my offices in the Antonia Praetorium here in Jerusalem not later than two weeks prior to the celebration of the Jewish Passover.

Alexander Gaius, Tribune"

The aging Roman sat back in his chair and mused:

"What an assignment! What he wouldn't give to be young enough to do it himself!"

"Will that be all, Sir?"

Gaius opened his eyes and realized that the Greek still awaited his next order.

"Yes, Scribe. Dispatch those orders immediately to the garrison at Caesarea Philippi. If the rider departs by noon today, he should be at the fort within seventy two hours."

CHAPTER NINE

When the Courier arrived at the Philippi Garrison some three and a half days later, he presented himself to the Centurion at the garrison office with an official communication and another letter directed to Lady Gaius.

Cassius accepted the official communication eagerly and looked up as the Courier said,

"I have a letter for Lady Gaius, Sir. Shall I deliver it to her?"

"Oh - no need. I will see that she gets it immediately. Thank you."

The Courier handed the letter to Cassius and, saluting said:

"I will return to Jerusalem at noon the day after tomorrow. I will report to you first, Centurion, in case you have any return messages or instructions."

Returning the salute, Cassius said,

"Good. Thank you."

The man moved off toward the garrison stables leading his weary horse.

Cassius turned and started across the Courtyard toward the Gaius apartment just as Lea stepped outside with a basket of trash.

"Lea.." Cassius called and, as she turned toward him, he continued:

"..I have a message here for Lady Gaius - from Jerusalem. Could you....?"

"Oh, yes, Sir. Thank you." She trotted toward him and, taking the letter from him, curtsied, then turned and hurried back to the apartment and up the stairs.

Back in the office, Cassius hurriedly unrolled the official communication and started to read.

Finished, he dropped the parchment and stared into space, stunned with the realization of what was ahead of him. Although, in its entirety, the responsibility of preparation, travel and his personal evaluation of another man, was hard to absorb and fully understand at this moment, one thing was certain. These orders would alter drastically his days and even the course of his life for some time to come.

That evening Portia leaned against the trunk of `their' tree, with the great coat spread out beneath her and waited for Cassius. The full moon this night flooded the rest of the garden but Portia was concealed in deep shadow. Shortly there was the scuffing sound of Cassius making his climb over the garrison wall and then the thud of his feet as he landed. When he ducked under the branches Portia was waiting and wrapped her arms around him and snuggled her face against his.

"Hello, darling," he whispered as he kissed her. As they sat down, he asked,

"You did get your letter from Jerusalem, didn't you?"

"Oh, yes. A nice letter. Gaius is lonesome after only such a short time. He wants me to come on to Jerusalem. I have already written a note telling him that it will be later, because I am not feeling well enough at the moment. I'll bring the note over to you in the morning. Did you get your expected orders?"

"Yes, I'll tell you...but first a hug, if you don't mind."

"Don't mind at all...I've been waiting all day for it."

He roughly grabbed her to him and their lips met in a hard, passionate kiss. When he felt that he could breathe again, he pulled himself a little bit away from her to ask,

"Tell me...you said you told him you didn't feel well. Are you really sick?!"

"No...I don't think so. The nausea comes and goes. Frankly, I think I am just worn out with the `night life'. She giggled, then:

"Now tell me about your news."

At the moment they were lying back on their cloak but as he started to speak he propped himself up on his elbow and looked down at her. His voice was soft, low and intent as he spoke.

"Well, the exciting part is the good part. I am to go to work on a disguise, growing my hair and a beard ... turning myself into a Jew, actually. Then travel down to Capernaum or wherever to find this Jesus and go along with these people who follow him. It will mean mingling and listening and watching all he does. The idea is to find out for the Romans whether he is a threat to Rome and its control over the people of Palestine...and so on."

"Well, I must say that sounds interesting enough..but how will you go about this disguise bit?"

"Well, first I can't shave and must grow my hair. That will take a bit longer and then...well, I talked to Lea`s Dan this afternoon. He is the chief gardener for this place we are in, you know!~

"Yes, I know. Go on."

"Well, after that I report to the Tribune and Pontius Pilate in Jerusalem where I am to remain....that's the bad part..for me anyway!"

"And me! I will certainly do everything possible to get to Jerusalem then!.

"Well, Portia there is so much to do and think about. One thing for which I *am* grateful is the study of the Aramaic language I have been doing. Another thing..please understand if I can't be here each evening. You will understand, won't you?"

"Of course, my Love!" With that she reached up and touched his face, let her hand run down his arm as she tugged at it. Quickly - eagerly, he dropped down beside her and wrapped both arms around her in a passionate embrace. Predictably they were enraptured with one another and time slipped by.

At length Portia gently pushed him away.

"I - I must go in, now, My Love. I am not feeling too well and just a bit..tired?

He snuggled into her neck, laughing softly.

"An understatement for both of us, I think."

On their feet, he sent her on her way and again went over the wall.

It was not as late as usual as Portia crawled into bed and she was grateful that she had enough know-how with the buckets to fix a little bath for herself, for she was clean and refreshed. Sleep claimed her quickly. The next morning she awoke to the sound of rain drops. Tip-toeing to the balcony, she looked up at the sky and relished the coming day. It was surprising - the rain - because last night the sky had been so clear. Whatever, it was a good excuse to lie abed and day-dream , which is what she did.

Pondering the surprising news she had received from Cassius, tears came to her eyes. Their times together from now until he had to leave would be especially precious. From what he said, there would be fewer times and time itself was short.

Listening to the rain and thinking how short their time now was, frightened her. When would she see him again and where, after he had left the Garrison? Everything would be different and she would be all alone. Gaius came to her mind but it was no comfort for now their relationship was of no consequence...with him she would still be alone. Suddenly beset by a spell of nausea, she dashed to the bathroom.

Back in bed again she asked herself for the hundredth time "What is this crazy sickness?"

There was a knock at the door and when she called out:

"Come in", Lea entered with the breakfast tray.

This was no help for it sent her dashing for the bathroom again. Lea frowned, bent down and smoothed the bed and as Portia re-entered the room,

"Lady Gaius, please come back to bed and just rest today. Your week of sewing has finally put your wardrobe in order and there is nothing pushing you. I don't like these nausea spells. What do you suppose they are?"

"I don't know. I don't like them either....I think I'll just play sick. Maybe, it will help. I can just sit here and dawdle at my needlework...and sleep when the mood hits. How does that sound?"

"Just fine. Now, you ring for me if you need anything at all and I'll go so you don't even have to talk."

"Thank you."

With Lea gone, Portia fell asleep and the needlework dropped to the floor.

Several days were identically the same. Evenings? Portia would bundle up, for the evenings were chilly, and go to the garden and wait on the bench for awhile. On the second night, Cassius came over the wall. Looking at him closely as he held her in his arms, Portia turned his head this way and that studying the beard and hair growth and frowned.

"Don't like it. It doesn't look like you...but I suppose that doesn't matter."

"Well, it matters, but is of no consequence because it has to be. Dan is getting me a wig. By the time I have that, I think I can leave. He already has clothes for me and the head covering. As soon as the beard itself is good enough, I will go because it is quicker than I thought it would be...this disguise bit. I will need all the time possible for the assignment."

Portia pouted, took his hand and tugged at him as she made her way through the orchard to `their` corner. As rested as she was there was no restraining her this night and their lovemaking was a thing of delight to Cassius. He picked her up in his arms as he sat up on their cloak and held her like a baby. Rocking back and forth, he tweaked at her breasts. She cried laughingly:

"Ouch!"

"What's the matter, Love?"

"They hurt!"

"Why?"

"I wish I knew."

"Well...that's no answer! For that I will send you off to bed -- it could be late, but let's look at the sky."

He gently pushed her off his lap and as he rose to his feet, pulled her to him. With a loving pat on her bottom. he pushed her out of the tree cavern and they looked at the sky....There was a brightening to the East.

"No, it is not late...it is early!"

"Ohhh...I must go! Brrrr..it's cold!"

He helped her into her tunic and warm cloak and put on his own. With a quick kiss he shoved her toward the gate and he dashed for the wall. He was into the Baths before anyone else and even had time for about an hour's nap. As for Portia, reaching the bathroom, she brought up a bucket or two, washed and flew into bed and off to sleep.

A couple of hours later when Lea entered cautiously, having received no answer to her knock, she smiled amusedly. It seemed to her that Portia was sleeping a great deal more than she ever had. Every day she seemed to come alive about time for lunch! Whatever did she do in the evenings that made her so sleepy? Nothing in the room gave Lea a clue and she shrugged to herself as she again pulled the drapes to shut out the brightening sunlight, placed the tray of breakfast fruit on the little table next to the balcony entrance and quietly left the room.

A short time later Portia awoke, stretched and put her feet on the floor. Looking over at the little table, she smiled. Lea had been here. Quickly she dashed to the table and, wide awake now, began to eat her breakfast.

A short time later, when Lea re-entered the room she was surprised to see Portia dressed in her `balloon,'pants as she called them, and a light weight wooly blouse.

"Well, Lady Gaius, did you get the sleep out of your system? You look very perky this morning."

"I had a wonderful sleep and woke up with a yen to go walk and climb around on our neighboring mountain with a picnic! How does that sound?"

"Fine. If you are up to it...fine."

"Well, I would like to try anyway. So far I have kept my breakfast down this morning."

"All right. I will go fix us a simple lunch snack and we can go anytime."

The hike didn't last too long. Portia's "feeling good" seemed to disappear with the effort at climbing and Lea was not at all averse to calling the whole thing off. So back they went, to the apartment.The time seemed to crawl and fly at the same time. Portia yearned for the nights to meet Cassius; and when he didn't appear, her tears did. The time of waiting was emotional and fearful all at once. It was much the same for Cassius, for his beard grew faster than he had thought it would and the thought of leaving Portia became something he dreaded facing. He forced himself to stay away from the garden for several nights simply to try to do without Portia...he could not face being without her and he had to try to get used to it or realize what it meant. The assignment awaited, and he could not avoid it.

He decided on the day he would leave which was in three days. For the two nights preceding he was with Portia until the small hours of the morning.

When Portia made her nightly visit to the garden on the third night she found a stranger standing on the path in front of the orchard. She stopped.

"Oh, I didn't know we had anyone visiting the Garrison, Sir. I am sorry to disturb you."

"You are not disturbing me, M'Lady."

It was Cassius' voice!

"Oh, My Love, what a marvelous disguise. I would never have guessed it was you!"

"That is what I wanted to hear, now --"

He snatched off the head-gear, wig and all.

Dropping them onto the bench, he held out his arms. She ran to him and he grabbed her, holding her very close...and tilting her chin up with his finger.

"I love you, Portia...with all of me there is to love."

"And I love you...for always."

They kissed, for a long and precious moment. She leaned her head back to look into his face. Within herself she knew something was about to happen that she didn't want to face. Taking his hand and turning, she attempted to lead him into the orchard. He did not move, but drew her back to face him.

"Portia dear, this is goodbye. It is better this way. A quick break will hurt us each a lot less."

She opened her mouth to speak, and he closed it with his own, in a long farewell kiss. Breaking from her, he - in one swift movement, had snatched up his wig and headgear and dashed to the outer wall.

She stood paralyzed as he climbed the wall, turning for a brief moment to look at her and say,

"Goodbye, darling. I love you. Take care of you for me."

And with that, he dropped to the ground on the other side.

Quickly, she called,

"And I love you. Please be careful...and goodbye, My Love."

He heard her and blew a farewell kiss toward the Garden.

The next morning Lea made what had become her usual quiet entrance to the bedroom and tiptoed to the bedside. What she saw brought a frown. Portia, sound asleep, was breathing with small hiccuppy sounds like sobs and her face was puffed with crying....and the pillow was wet when Lea's finger smoothed a wrinkle. What had happened?! What was wrong?! With her customary wisdom, she just shrugged and quietly left the room, knowing intuitively that Portia would confide in her if she could.

CHAPTER TEN

Feeling the dread of leaving all of life that had any meaning for him, Cassius walked with determined tread through the cool of evening, took the reins from Helmut's hand, and mounted his horse. Helmut led the small ass which was packed with Cassius' needs for living off the land. Portia was only a short distance away, but at some point, he must put her out of his mind and focus on the strange assignment before him.

`Find Jesus'? `Walk with his followers, then meet with Tribune Gaius before the Passover in Jerusalem?'..such were the thoughts coursing through his brain.

He turned to Helmut.

"Have you ever made the trip from the Garrison to Capernaum~?

"Yes, sir. It's not a long trip, and it's downhill all the way from here. You'll be pleased too, I think, with the fact that it's much warmer."

"Whatever. Let's go down this mountain and, if possible, find a site to camp before too far into the night."

Helmut sensed his irritation and wondered what strange assignment the Centurion could have that not only permitted him to appear unshaven and unkempt but also required him to work alone.

The trail descended to the West and then South. Cassius remembered their journey up the same trail and the awful fatigue after they reached the Garrison. That seemed like years ago, for his life had changed so from that day. Just so did the harsh mountain terrain give way at the end just below the garrison where the headwaters of the Jordan burst from the earth in a beautiful falls. It was probably here that Philip, the third of Herod's sons, fell in love with the land of Paneas which he renamed Caesarea Philippi and claimed for his own. Here the Jordan began and continued to give to this part of the world beauty, bounty, and the lush greenery which seemed to calm men's souls.   Cassius remembered their crossing the Jordan Valley in their trip up from Tyre and his own enchantment. So it was that this trip began to promise a few good points. They camped within sound of the Falls.

Cassius and Helmut rode their horses along the road leading into Capernaum, paying little heed to the inquiring looks from those walking the same road. Cassius was well into his guise of Jew with luxuriant black beard covering much of his face, while his skullcap with four-cornered shawl and tassels covered black, curly hair not yet long enough to be convincing. The image, however, was believable enough to be disconcerting to those who knew that Jews did not ride horses.

When they had ridden well into the afternoon, they approached a town.

"Is this Capernaum?" Cassius asked.

"No, Sir. This is just Chorazin. However, it's not much further now to Capernaum. Will you wish me to stay the night with you?"

"It may be longer than that. I will dismount shortly and walk the rest of the way. You will make camp for us among those trees which obviously border the river; and I hope that you are a good cook. I'm hungry already, and I suspect that my walk into town will not make it any better. I'll be back by nightfall and meet you by that boulder there next to the cedar."

"Your camp will be ready as will your evening meal, Sir."

Helmut smiled with the implicit questioning of his ability to cook.   The Centurion did not know that he had taken a substantial portion of roasted beef from the garrison larder; warming it over the   coals would be a delicious surprise..especially so when washed down with the wine cooled in its wineskin in the waters of the Jordan.

Cassius' mind was on a different tack, having dismissed the matter of the camp.

"I hope this rabbi Jesus is in Capernaum. Finding him is the first part of our assignment, though I haven't the faintest idea of how one would find him if he's not here in town."

Helmut was utterly surprised..

"You are looking for Jesus, Sir?"

"Yes. Is that so unusual?"

"Well, I would believe it odd. You see, from what I have heard, those with incurable diseases and others with strange concern for the Jewish Religion seem to be ones looking for him. You don't seem to be either."

Cassius smiled and realized that Helmut would just have to continue to wonder.

Walking into town was a welcome change from the saddle. He followed the other travelers into the market place. Perhaps the vendor of some of those succulent figs would also have some knowledge of the itinerant rabbi. As he approached one of the larger stalls, he heard the irate voice of the owner berating a hapless employee.

"Offal of pigs!" the bigger man shouted. "Not even you could be that stupid!" The merchant grasped the garment of his slave and shoved him against a wall where he cowered with expectancy of further physical abuse.

"Do you have a problem?" Cassius asked, realizing almost too late that he was no longer a Roman Officer but just another Jew.

The merchant dropped his slave and turned, possibly expecting to see someone in authority. Seeing only the well-dressed Jew did nothing to please him.

"So, who are you?"

"Just one in need of your excellent produce. I was hoping that I would not be too late in the day to buy figs for our table."

The merchant observed the quality of Cassius' clothing and his bearing of implicit authority. Perhaps more than an ordinary Jew.

"You are not too late. And you are right. My produce is the best available."

Cassius made his purchase, paid the man, and asked:

"Do you know of a rabbi named Jesus? He is said to live here in Capernaum."

Ali ben Aboud chuckled. So *that* was why this stranger accosted him.

"Jesus does not live here. In fact, he seems to move about a great deal. We have many coming to Capernaum seeking him.~

"Is he here now?"

"I do not know, of course. I have heard that he and his followers are in Perea."(1)

Seeing that nothing more could be learned of the Arab, Cassius started to walk back to the campsite and Helmut. He noted the chill of the evening and looked forward to the warmth of the campfire.

Helmut was waiting as he had been directed. Other travelers were also in their area, but Helmut had secured a niche between two large boulders which would afford them both shelter from any winds and privacy for sleeping.

"Is the rabbi in Capernaum?" he asked.

"No. I am told that he has gone to Perea. Do you know the area?"

"Not well. It's on the East side of the Jordan with Gadara probably being the largest town."

"How far is it from here?"

"A full day's ride, I would believe."

Cassius weighed the feasibility of riding versus walking inasmuch as the former
would entail being noticed more than he wished to be. Still, if he walked, the rabbi might move away further still.

"We will ride then -- at dawn." The Centurion ate hungrily and slept as well as he could. The need for Portia in every way that he could think of was like a constant flame within him. Even so, he was tired, and he slept.

The next morning, rather than continue Southward through Magdala and Tiberius, Helmut and Cassius skirted the North side of the Sea of Galilee and then followed the road on the Eastern shore which led to Gadara. Both were amazed with the number of people walking in the same direction. Perhaps one or two rode camels, but they alone were on horses.

"I might just as well wear sign saying, `This is a Roman'," Cassius reflected. So be it. Time was of the essence.

As they rode on and encountered multitudes on the road, he asked:

(1) New Testament, Gospel of John, Ch. 10.

"Is it usually like this, Helmut? We have seen Parthians, Syrians, Jews and what-not today

"I think not, Centurion. There are many rumors about this rabbi, some of which may be true. I suspect that many of these on the way are seeking him for reasons of their own."

The possibility of actually finding Jesus suddenly made Cassius acutely aware of his appearance. Would he pass, or would someone suspect that he was other than just another of the rabble?

"How do I look, Helmut?"

"More like the others of this region than I would have believed possible when we were at the Garrison, Sir. You certainly would fool me if I didn't know you."

"Good, I suppose," Cassius replied.

As they neared Gadara, the number of travelers became even more numerous. What kind of man would attract such a following? They surely must be getting closer to this rabbi.

"Let's pull up here, Helmut. I don't want to stand out, so take the horses and return to Caesarea Philippi. Report to my replacement there at the garrison. You have no further duty for me other than to return as soon as possible. You are not to discuss either my appearance or our quest for the rabbi. Is that understood?"

As Helmut answered in the affirmative, Cassius realized that not only had he left Portia and a whole way of life behind but he would now lose the one person he knew in this wilderness.

"I'll be back as soon as I can, Helmut. But what I have to do will take weeks at least."

Helmut handed the reins of the burro to Cassius. He wondered how well his master would fare, what he was doing here, and what could determine when he could come home again. Not his place to ask. With a crisp salute, he mounted his horse, took Hunter's reins, and began his return to the fort.

The afternoon sun was warmer than one would expect for this time of the year, and Cassius regretted that he had no choice other than to continue on foot as did everyone else. He noted, however, that the well-dressed traveler in front of him seemed to wander a bit from side to side as he walked. Suddenly, he staggered, fell, and dropped the light pack that he had been carrying. Cassius dropped the burro's reins, and he stopped as he had been trained to do.

As the stranger struggled to regain his feet, Cassius helped him up and said:

"Hold onto me, and we'll get into the shade of that tree. "

The man held on, saying nothing. Cassius parked him then under a tree and poured water from his canteen onto a towel. He offered it to the man who silently wiped his hands and face. The Centurion then took out one of his succulent figs from his pack and said:

"Here. Eat this. You'll fell better when you have rested." The Traveler looked at him owlishly with some suspicion.

"Where are you from? Your speech is not usually heard in Jerusalem."

"I am Elias ben Joseph,. My family is in Siracusa. Why do you ask?"

"It is not my custom to accept either food or kindness from strangers. In this case, I have no choice. I have been ill and thought that I had recovered. Obviously, I have not. I am expected at a dinner in Gadara given by my uncle Nicodemus, and I am making every effort to be there for rather special reasons."

"Oh?" said Cassius. "Though I have no thought as to your 'special reasons', I too wish to be in Gadara. There is a rabbi named Jesus who is supposed to be there, and I am at a disadvantage in that I have never been to that city."

"Why do you wish to see Jesus?"

"Let us say, as you did, that I too have 'special reasons.' I suppose that everyone who has the time would love to know more about a man who seems to attract people from everywhere."

"Yes, he does at that. My name is Ephraim. This Jesus is to be a guest at a dinner in Gadara. He is almost certain to be a fraud, though we'll see. Would you like to come as my guest? My brother was to come, but he is in Rome."

Cassius could scarcely believe his ears. What good luck!

"Will you not be censored for bringing a stranger to your

uncle's dinner?"

"Actually, no. My family and the rest of the Sanhedrin are a bit uncertain of Nicodemus in that he would invite this fellow in the first place and that he seems to approve of him in the second. That I have decided to come is a favor to him, and he will not question your being with me. However, if we are to be there, and the dinner is to be tomorrow, we'd better get going."

"You are not in the best of condition to be continue to walk. I'll be pleased to place your small pack with mine on the ass, and you at least will not have to carry anything. Where will you sleep tonight?"

"I will sleep in my uncle's house. Again, you are welcome to stay as my guest. Your beast of burden will be fed and sheltered in the stable." Ephraim chuckled then, something that Cassius suspect to be a rarity.

"At least, this way, I am assured to getting there!"

The rest of the trip was made without incident, though Ephraim seemed slightly nauseated from his malaise. When they arrived at Nicodemus' house, Cassius was astounded to find this secondary residence to be of such opulence. (Ephraim had said that Nicodemus usually lived in Jerusalem.) Cassius, alias Elias of Siracusa, was assigned to a beautifully furnished room with a servant to prepare his bed, attend his bathing in a hot pool, and provide him with sleeping attire -- because his own was still unpacked. Sleep came blissfully, though his thoughts were haunted with Portia. He wondered whether she might still be ill with her strange stomach upset.

Breakfast consisted of melon and hotcakes, but it was apparent that one was expected to eat lightly until dinner. Cassius was feeling well fed and greatly rested, though he was ill at ease with the thought of the careful scrutiny that he would get when he met his host. One having the kind of wealth manifest in this house would certainly be nobody's fool!

"When will we meet your uncle, Ephraim?"

"I'm not sure....perhaps after dinner today. He is busy with his other guests and particularly with this wandering rabbi who also spent the night." Cassius felt yet another reprieve, though Ephraim seemed to accept his story without question.

His room servant approached quietly and said:

"Dinner is served, Master. Please come with me."

Cassius felt conspicuous in being seated near the head table, though Ephraim seemed to feel confident of their placement. He had scarcely been seated when members of the Sanhedrin arrived with the pageantry of their importance. Each was seated with great obsequiousness, and each seemed to accept his treatment as if it were due him. There were five of them all told. And though each was distinctive, all were of dark complexion and that greatly in contrast to the next guest to arrive. He was of Cassius' approximate age. His hair was of almost a golden blonde color, while his skin was scarcely darker than a deep tan. (1)

"Is that Jesus?" Cassius queried.

"Yes, that's your `rabbi'. We have long been suspicious of his coloration, but his mother exhibits the same reddish hue."

The ritual of blessing the bread over with, food was served..indeed, platters of fowl and lamb, together with the sweet vegetables grown in the lush valley.

Cassius finished his wine and last mouthful when Ephraim whispered -

"Now watch this. Our so-called rabbi is about to be exposed. A fellow, who was obviously not dressed as the others..in fact, he looked quite shabby..spoke up suddenly:

"Rabbi!"

Jesus looked up, quite possibly embarrassed, because so may rabbis were present that his answering would have been at least in bad taste.

"Rabbi!" the man called again. "If you will, I can be healed."

Looking closely, Cassius saw that the man was terribly bloated. Dark circles under his eyes seems filled with fluid, and his limbs were so edematous that he could only stand with one supporting him on either side. Obviously, Jesus saw the same thing, a man terminally ill with congestive cardiac insufficiency.

Jesus stood then and, looking to his left down the row of elite guests asked:

1) *Pilate's Report: The Archko Volume, Keats Publishing, New Canaan, Conn.

"Is it lawful to heal on the Sabbath?" (1)

Saying nothing more then to anyone, Jesus walked to the poor man. He placed one hand on his shoulder; and, lifting his other hand as if in the air, he prayed quietly so that Cassius could not hear his words. There was then no sound in the room until it rang with the words of the sick man.

Shouting words of praise to Yahweh, the man stared incredulously at his hands and then his feet. Then he fell to his knees and kissed the hands of Jesus who raise him to his feet and pushed him gently toward the door.

"Incredible! He cured him on the *Sabbath!*" Ephraim whispered. "That man was terminally ill with Dropsy."

Jesus turned then to face the elite guests at the head table.

"Which of you, having a donkey or an ox fallen into a pit, will not immediately pull him out on a Sabbath day?"(1)

No one responded. There were no answers.

Cassius was still savoring the incredible cure of the man with dropsy, but the cure seemed to be of less interest to Ephraim.

"He cured him on *The Sabbath!*

Lest he expose his ignorance of the matter, Cassius remained silent while his host explained:

"To work on the Sabbath is clearly an infraction of the Mosaic Law!" Then Cassius noticed the agitation among the Sanhedrin group. But despite fervent gesticulation and bobbing of heads, nothing was said to Jesus.

"This whole thing seemed to be contrived..planned to get Jesus to break the law. Was that the case, Ephraim?"

"Obviously. Jesus has long been contending that he is the Son of God and other abominable claims as well. Getting that shabby wretch over here to get Jesus to cure him even required payment before he would come. Even he didn't believe that he could be cured!"

"Well, if he broke a law, why hasn't someone had him arrested ?"

(1)   New Testament, Gospel of Luke, Ch.14, v.3
(2)New Testament, Chapter 14, vss.1-14.

Ephraim smiled.

"How can we arrest a man who so obviously tells the truth? None of us could cure the man of dropsy, but any one of us would have pulled our donkey out of a ditch. What could we say?"

Jesus seemed to be enjoying the situation. He looked at the elite group so carefully seated at the head table, each according to his social standing and began an address obviously intended to shame them all.

"When you are invited by anyone to a wedding feast, do not sit down in the best place.." (1)

To Cassius' astonishment, Jesus proceeded to chastise the Pharisees which was the name by which Ephraim had identified the group. Was there anything here of political ambition? Jesus had just performed a medical miracle, but could he get away with insulting his host's guests? Apparently he could, for someone at the head table..probably Nicodemus..said:

"Blessed is he who shall eat bread in the Kingdom of God." (2)

None of this interested Cassius so much as the obvious political implication. Plainly, Jesus couldn't have cared less about political popularity!

The dinner ended abruptly with almost all of those at the head table walking out with scarcely a backward glance. Only one remained with Jesus. Cassius turned to his host.

"Thank you, Ephraim. I have never seen anything at all like any of this, and it is apparent that your uncle is still busy. Please thank him for me. The afternoon is getting late, and I have yet to secure a place to spend the night."

"And your `special reasons'..has your purpose been served here?"

"More than you know. Thank you again." Cassius went to the stable and strapped his pack again onto his burro. As he emerged to leave Gadara, he found that hundreds of people had been waiting for Jesus to come out of the house. He was surrounded and moved with his disciples helping to make a path

(1 & 2) New Testament, Gospel of Luke, Ch14.

90

for him. Having no other commitment, Cassius remained with the crowd as they pushed their way into the countryside. Jesus himself must also have been tired, because he continued to walk with disciples toward the wide clearing near the road which would accommodate the multitude as a suitable place to camp and spend the night.

The sun was getting low in the West when they arrived at the clearing that Cassius had noted when he had passed only yesterday. The crowd stopped respectfully when the disciples turned, joined hands, and formed a human barrier. Obviously, Jesus needed privacy and a chance to rest.

Cassius led his burro to an area well to one side of the road and on the lee side of the hill. Removing the pack from the animal, he found a nose bag and oats which had been packed for the purpose of feeding him as he did now. No one had ever told him the beast's name, and so he named the small critter "Horse:, a ridiculous choice but humor suited him in the late afternoon. While "Horse" munched his oats, Cassius rolled out his bedroll and built a small fire to prepare his own dinner. A small stream close by splashed and gurgled over the stones in its bed, and Cassius availed himself the luxury of the fresh cold water.

"Do you come this way often?"

Cassius was startled to see the other man who had also chosen this site by the stream. The stranger was not as tall as he, a bit older, and reminded him somehow of an oak.

"No, I've not been here before. Am I intruding on your camp?"

"Not at all. My name is Simon, and I'm pleased to have your company."

Cassius had the strange feeling that meeting Simon here and now was not really a coincident at all. But how could it have been otherwise?

"I am Elias. You might have noticed as others have that my Aramaic has a Grecian flavor. My family is in Siracusa."

Simon's smile seemed close to laughter, though again, Cassius could not put a finger on it.

Simon said then:

"Would you join me in eating these fish? I seem to have caught more than I can eat; and, on the other hand, I certainly don't want to tell any of that hungry mob of my good fortune."

"Thank you. I've enough wine left for the two of us, bread baked just before I left, and sweet cakes which I believe you'll like."

Cassius had learned to be cautious in the presence of strangers, but Simon had a way of putting him at ease. It was unusual, however, for this man to be here by the stream completely alone and particularly so, if he were a part of the Rabbi's followers.

"We all seem to be following this Jesus today. You seem healthy enough, though, so I would guess that you just happen to be on the road at the same time. Are you among the followers?"

"Yes, you might say that I am a follower. In fact, I am a disciple; but, unlike the others, I need to be alone occasionally. Why are you here?"

Simon's directness was disturbing. Young and certainly in ebullient good health, Cassius' presence did indeed require a sensible answer.

"The best answer that I can give is that I am looking for something, something which perhaps I can find here. I want to listen and learn."

"You have traveled this far out into the wilderness, left your family in Greece, and come out here..'looking for something'?"

The Centurion realized that he was cornered. He could easily have told Simon to leave it at that, or he could have pursued some other evasive answer. Instead, he chose just to be silent and wait.

"Maybe you'd like to meet Jesus?" Simon queried.

"No, not yet. As I said, I do want to listen and learn. There is so much that I want to know and so much that confuses me. I saw the miracle yesterday with my own eyes; and I saw, at the same time, that Jesus profaned the Sabbath. Could you explain these things to me?"

"Maybe I could, Elias. Maybe I could. But the truth, the answers that really matter, you will have to find for yourself. For now, I must sleep. Good night, Elias of Siracusa."

Cassius was alone now by the fire and more lonely than he could ever remember. But finding Simon could be the best thing yet, though prying information out of him could be like milking a stone.

CHAPTER ELEVEN

Within a day or so, a stranger arrived accompanied by an Auxiliary who had originally left the Philippi Garrison with Gaius. The stranger was Dr. Tibius. The first Portia knew of their arrival was when they walked onto the portico outside the office. She was sitting on the edge of the fountain pool in the courtyard of the building.

First they went into the office and then Claudius, who had taken Cassius place to supervise the Garrison, came out with the stranger and indicated Portia at the fountain. The stranger moved toward the fountain and Portia looked up as he approached:

"May I help you, Sir?"

"Lady Gaius?"

"Yes."

"Lady Gaius, I am Dr. Anthony Tibius by name, sent by Tribune Gaius to look into the state of your health."

Portia was at a loss..."The state of my health?"

"You sent a message to the Tribune stating you were not well..."

"Oh, yes -- now I remember. And, truly, Doctor, I - I am not just exactly feeling like me. I guess that is one way of saying it."

"Not a bad way, really..but with a few questions and an examination, I am sure I can help solve the puzzle. Is there a place we may talk and so forth, Lady Gaius?"

"Yes, my private quarters. However, Doctor, you are surely weary and would like to clean up first. Why don't we get you settled?"

"Well...now, perhaps that is a good idea."

"Wait here just a moment." Portia hurried to the office and came out with Claudius who beckoned for the Doctor to follow him.

Dr. Tibius turned toward Portia with a smile,

"I will see you later, my Dear?"

"Yes, of course."

Portia, waiting for Dr. Fabius' arrival at the Gaius apartment was beset by a series of conflicting emotions because of the fact that, by now, she was acutely aware that all symptoms indicated an extreme change in her life. The realization of the very real possibility that she was carrying Cassius' child stirred her love into the most agonized state of longing she could ever have imagined. At the same time she was frightened. If she was right and the Doctor confirmed her thinking, he was going to return to Alex with the diagnosis. What would happen then..what would be Alex' reaction?

Her mind flashed back to the night before Alex was to leave, and their lovemaking. It was possible that this was Alex' baby, although nothing of this nature had ever occurred in their marriage. Confident that the child was Cassius', she had to persuade herself that it *was* Alex's baby. It *had* to be! No one dare know or suspect the truth.

She did not know, of course, that Gaius would know the truth, which would not only affect her life but Cassius' life as well.

Dr. Tibius arrived and, after a brief examination and a few pertinent questions, confirmed Portia's suspicions.

"Why have you not confided this great joy to your husband, Lady Gaius?"

"No reason. For a bit of time I wasn't aware or, rather, paid little heed to symptoms. I was too busy finishing the business of getting settled and Alex was not here, having left for Jerusalem...sooo"

"Well,surely his not being here is reason enough. Shall I advise him when I return? He will want to know, Lady Gaius, my diagnosis."

"No. No, let me write him a letter to send with you which you can hand to him when he asks you. Will that do, do you suppose?"

"I can see nothing wrong with it. I will rest from the horse tomorrow and give the beast a chance at me the next day. That should give you time."

"Thank you, Doctor Tibius. Incidentally, will you do me the

honor of dining with me this evening, here in the apartment?"

"I would be delighted, Madame, thank you."

Portia felt a sense of reprieve for the hours given her to compose a proper letter to Alex.

The task seemed impossible, for it involved the melding of two utterly incompatible worlds. As she considered it, objectively she hoped, the first realm was one defying a clear definition. Her garden was, or had been when Cassius was there, enchantment. Their love-making built from intensity to bone-quaking response in their mutual orgasm and then she lived in a kind of quiet ecstasy. Her roses smelled of an almost pungent sweetness. The songs of birds, not usually noticed, were clear in the morning, and the small stream coursing through the garden gurgled its own joyous soliloquy. Clearly, there was no relationship of that experience to the down to earth living with Gaius which made up the second realm. The beginning was not marked. It just was. In her joy, she asked how could these two utterly different worlds exist together? Now, the coming of the baby forced necessity, and she must choose inexorable reality. Cassius was gone in that seemingly calloused way that men have when they choose between duty over love. If he had any thoughts of permanence in their relationship, certainly he had never mentioned it. And wouldn't it be ironic if, by some miracle, she could extricate herself from this marriage just when she had conceived Gaius' child after wanting for so long to have a baby? Not only was the necessity of choice cruel; but, for the first time in her life, she had to deceive..at least, be deceptive of what she herself wanted so desperately. The letter must be written and perhaps a whole lifetime of deception begun. And so she did.

"Dearest Alex,

Thank you for having sent Dr. Tibius. He was so kind, and his wonderful discovery made my misery worth it all. Things I should have known but didn't, he explained ever so patiently.

As you know, my mother died when I was a baby, and Pappa raised me with the help of a nanny and women servants. He did well, as fathers go, and Nanny left while I was still just a girl. So, it was a friend, Petula, who explained the girl thing when I became a young woman. But none of that helped with sickness which plagued me before Dr. Tibius came. He explained the tiredness and my stomach upsets. We are going to have a baby!

I have wanted for the years of our marriage to be a mother, and so Dr. Tibius' diagnosis was such a wonderful surprise! I am thrilled! But I do have some concerns.

You know, each time I have tried to talk with you about our becoming parents, you have changed the subject, said nothing, or just gone to sleep. And so, you have never really told me how you would feel about being a father, though it has always seemed to me that you would be as wonderful as a father as you are as a husband.

I am thrilled, and I love you so for making me happy, even though you couldn't have known until now. Dr. Tibius will be delivering my letter, but I wanted so to tell you myself instead of his giving you just a cold diagnosis. Hopefully, I will feel like the trip to Jerusalem soon. The doctor said I should feel better after the first three months, so we shall see!

So, for now, goodbye, Alex Dear.

Love, Portia"

She couldn't know at the moment whether the nausea she felt was the baby's fault or her own revulsion with the lies.

The next day the Doctor left for Jerusalem with her letter. Standing by the fountain she watched him ride away and promptly fell into a spell of grief which was to last a lifetime. The most unbearable agony was the realization that she must put Cassius out of her mind...most important out of her heart. Forget she could not, but all remembrance must bury itself in the love of their child. Her eyes, her words, her actions could never reveal the truth if they met again.

Her role of wife and soon, mother, had to be played out to and for Alex. Cassius must return to the fantasy of "the hornblower".

Turning toward the apartment, Portia changed her mind and headed for the Garden. Once inside, seeing no one there, she ran to `their' tree in the orchard. Standing there, as in a dream for a few moments, she moved slowly toward the niche where the cloak was hidden. Clasping it to her heart she slowly returned through the orchard to the path leading to the outer wall. Stepping onto the bench, she tossed it to the other side of the wall. Back on the path she got as far as the bench next to the flowers where she sank down and began to sob.

Lea, having seen her enter the garden from the kitchen window, debated with herself for a little while and then making a quick decision, quietly left the kitchen with a basket on her arm. Opening the gate she stepped inside to see Portia crying and quickly moved to sit beside her on the bench. She did not speak, but Portia needed her and turned to her with a sob. Lea embraced her and held her as she cried.

Slowly, the sobbing subsided. Lea spoke softly.

"Is there anything I can do to help...?"

Portia mopped her face with her handkerchief and strove to control herself. Looking up with red and swollen eyes revealing her pain, she spoke haltingly...

"I don't know..."

"If...if I had any idea of what you needed...I could try.."

Portia, for one moment, wished for Claudia...then realized that as much as she loved Claudia...it would be wiser to have Lea to talk to. Her secret would be safe with Lea.

"Well...I need so to talk to someone...I feel so alone...it - it's a long story..."

"I - I am so fond of you, Lady Gaius...I would like so much to help."

"Well..Lea...we might as well begin to be best friends..and for that I need to be `Portia' to you...all right?"

"Of course...it will be hard to say Portia at first...but I will try..."

Portia smiled in the middle of a hiccup-sob and they both laughed a little bit.

Lea reached over and took hold of Portia's hand.

Slowly Portia began to tell her secret..in between a few tears and some sobs. Lea was astounded at how well Portia had kept her secret to herself...but the strange sleeping hours of weeks past and the sick spells were now so very clearly understood but the heartache the story revealed, was not something Lea was sure she could help...but she would comfort, at least. Finally, Portia stood up and put her arms around Lea and tears again ran down her face.

"Lea, I have to cry it out for awhile, I guess. But one thing I know...I must leave the Garden. I can't ever come back."

"I can understand that, Portia. I really can. Let's go now. We'll go upstairs and get you a bath and put you down for another early night....you need it."

Portia simply nodded and they left the garden.

Since that day with Lea, Portia had been lost in a depressed quandary of sadness and confusion and too much crying. At almost the same time Cassius was beginning his walk in Perea, she began to feel a sudden rebellion with her situation. Impatiently she faced her misery and determined to put it from her. She had known what she had to do but had hurt so much she could take no affirmative action -- now she must. She had to get on with living for the sake of the baby and prepare herself for Alex. He was a good man and really would be thrilled to be a father.

How could she begin? What could she do? Perhaps..She was hit with an idea. Claudia! The long planned trip back to Caesarea to see Claudia would keep her busy and change her thoughts! If the Games were on that would help and then -- then from there she could go on to Jerusalem before it would be too miserable for her to travel!

That was it...how wonderful that she had just received another letter from Claudia begging her to come. Dashing to her letter table to accept the invitation...and ask if she could stay for several weeks, she added a postscript.

"Don't answer...I am packing to come We'll probably leave in two days!"

She rang for Lea and when she arrived, handed her the letter.

"Honey, please run down and give this to Claudius so he can send it with today`s Courier and then come right back!"

Lea returned to find her tossing clothing onto the bed.

"Whatever are you doing.?"

"What you'll be doing, too. Getting ready to pack to go to

100

Caesarea and then, Lea, on to Jerusalem. You will go with me, of course. However, after Caesarea and the visit with Claudia, you might want to come back here...because of Dan, you know."

Lea was staring at her and her mind racing with her words. The visit to Caesarea would be fun. But Jerusalem? Portia would be staying, of course. But there *was* Dan. Then she remembered Dan`s words of just last night and how he wanted to get out of Caesarea Philippi and to Jerusalem. I wonder...she thought...then suddenly grinned.

"You have me all the way to Jerusalem, Portia. Dan wants to `shake the dust of this place' from his feet. He yens for Jerusalem...this may be just the way to help him."

"Oh, wonderful. We can have such fun. I can bet Dan bolts for Jerusalem." Portia hesitated, smiling.

"Lea, I want you with me always if possible. But don't cross off coming back if you want to. If Dan doesn't go for it - I know you love him, and..."

"Yes. I understand. But know I want to be with you too, Portia. And I hope calling you Portia isn't a problem...I know it isn't right. But you said..."

"It's no problem. I love it. I don't feel so all alone with you close to me."

She threw her arms around Lea and drew her close in a hug. Lea leaned back and grinned.

"Now, My Lady, we have to hustle. We have that crazy morning sickness of yours to work around, you know."

"Yes, I know."

"Now, you lie down for a rest. I'll go over to see Claudius and tell him of our plans, so he can get a travel team together to get us to Caesarea. We should be ready to travel in a couple days, I think. It will be different packing with the probability of a permanent move."

"You are right. We will need a good sized wagon and we can resurrect the tiny travel wagon I came up in, I should think."

Lea wore a wreath of smiles as she left the apartment. When the door closed, Portia felt completely apart from the self she had become. She let out an excited squeal and did a twirl which dizzied her and sent her hurrying for the bed. Lying there, she began to sort the packing problem out in her head. It didn't last long, for very shortly she had drifted off to the dreamless sleep of a mid-day nap.

She woke up to see Lea at the little table bent over busily writing with her pretty forehead wrinkled in a `thinking' frown.

"What has you so puzzled?" Portia asked.

Startled, Lea quickly turned her way.

"Ah, you're awake! Not really puzzled..just struggling to `work out' the things we can leave behind or discard, after which we can get rid of them. Then we can start packing in some sort of order. All right?"

"Yes..very all right. I would not have thought of that, myself and it surely does make sense!"

"Are you up to doing anything this afternoon, Portia?"

"Oh, yes. That nap made me feel all `new'!"

"My idea would be to tackle your wardrobe first..does that seem reasonable to you?"

"Very. It needs thinning anyway. Let's do it."

And so it began. Lea couldn't know why, of course, but the floor was suddenly littered with a collection of very nice short night time tunics and stollas that Portia identified with Cassius and their meetings. Everything she found that she had worn in his presence lay on the floor. Inside of her she was hurting so much that she finally dashed into the bathroom to splash water on her face and wash away sign of tears.   Lea made a perfectly normal comment as she began picking the garments up and folding them.

"These are so nice, I hate to throw them out. May I just bundle them and take them to the City for the poor?"

"Yes...that is a good idea. I will be in Caesarea and just go on a shopping spree! I need to boost my spirits anyway!!"

Totally unsuspecting, Lea smiled as she added, "I would think so and what a fun way to do it...shopping!"

With the most painful part of the packing process decided and done with, Portia could set to work with her mind on the matter and her emotions more or less stable. Their packing and deciding what to do with the household things they wanted, filled up the next day and a half...the rest of the time they got themselves together...travel clothes, etc. Happily, the apartment had been furnished and the few things transported from Rome, which they had never used anyway, Portia decided to donate to the apartment. So, right on schedule with time --as stated in her letter to Claudia, they were ready to travel the morning of the third day.

Dan had taken the time that they used packing to get his own life ready to move. The big wagon was quite full when time came to leave. Dan volunteered to drive that wagon which freed up the two Auxiliaries whom Claudius had assigned to the travel project. Petta, the cook who had come with the Gaius' from Rome, eagerly joined the travel group. The three women rode in the tiny travel wagon in which Portia had come from Caesarea. However, there was no feather bed! Each of the women had a nice, thick sleeping roll for night time. The pads fit quite nicely, side by side, across the wagon bed. A heavy tarp covered them and the travel seats were above so that two could ride there with the third guiding the team. Lea eagerly volunteered for this; however, Portia pleaded with her to share. It made her feel 'back home' so she said.

So it was that bright and early the morning of the third day after the big decision, the tiny caravan left Caesarea Philippi.Portia had reached the path at the foot of the stairs from the apartment and stood very still for just a moment on the path which also led to the garden gate. Her heart had pounded inside her as she turned to look at the garden gate. Just the sight of the gate had jarred her back into memory. Tears sprang into her eyes. It had taken great will power to push the pain down and turn her mind away...a discipline she was to get used to.

The first time it was very difficult. When she climbed into the little wagon, she was quiet. Lea turned from the driver seat to look closely at her. Catching her eye, Lea blew her a kiss. Portia smiled.

The trip to Caesarea began, following the route Cassius had taken, down through and across the Jordan Valley with its fruit and lush vegetation. Predictably, the girls stopped progress while they picked a large basket of fruit for the trip. Portia decided to follow the same route they had taken to come to

Philippi, traveling past the outskirts of Tyre and down the road closest to the sea. As she had remembered, the road was over mostly level ground, and the trip turned out to be fairly easy. It brought back memories that were pleasant and none of which were filled with Cassius.

Lea and Dan and Petta, basically being servants, were very much at ease with the Auxiliaries. At first the friendly ease felt strange to Portia..but not for long. The friendly chatter and laughter was catching and, truly, it was not long before the journey was fun-filled and happy and, incidentally, very good for Portia. When they arrived at the beautiful home overlooking the sea and but a short distance from the Garrison, one of the Auxiliaries quickly dismounted and hurried up the approach to the door. Claudia had been watching . The door opened, and she ran toward the little wagon to greet Portia who, at this moment was on the driver's seat. Claudia burst out laughing,

"What are you doing, Lady -- up there playing wagon master!?"

"Having fun, that's what!"

Portia, in her full, floppy trousers hopped down to grab Claudia in her arms for a big hug. And so the visit began.

Dan went to the Garrison with the Auxiliaries to arrange for a horse to travel to Jerusalem. They took the big wagon with its cargo into the protection of the garrison walls and left the little wagon for Portia to organize when she decided to go on to Jerusalem, at the Fabius stables.

It was getting toward evening when they arrived and Claudia made Dan promise to come back for dinner. Then the women went inside in a torrent of chatter. Lea and Petta carried their personal bundles of clothing, etc. to the room they were to share. Claudia and Portia carried her things to the room in which she and Gaius had stayed on their earlier arrival in the country. It was a joyful arrival and happy dinner hour. Dan announced he would take off early the next day and Lea went outside with him as he left to go to the garrison for the night.

Of course, Portia did not keep her condition any secret. Claudia was overjoyed, for which Portia was very grateful. It made the visit easy and fun. Portia explained to Claudia that being all alone, the only women in the garrison at Caesarea Philippi, she and Lea and Petta had become good friends, stressing the fact that to her they were helpful friends - not servants. This eliminated any difficulty of understanding when the three newcomers talked with each other and used first names. Claudia was not much for formality anyway, so the visit was certainly a blessing for both Lea and Petta after their years of tight protocol.

It was a wonderful two weeks..then three...then four. The Athletic Games at the Amphitheater had come and gone so there was plenty of walking at the beach and playing in the sea. Portia's morning sickness finally passed. Her slender figure was noticeably `swelling' and walking gracefully wasn't easy. One morning Claudia and Portia were sitting on the balcony overlooking the ocean. Finally, the mad and endless chatter that had peppered the days was disappearing. Genuine conversations regarding Portia's coming motherhood, life in Jerusalem and the coming day for departure held the floor. Today was one of those.

"Claudia, I must start planning on leaving for Jerusalem very soon."

"Oh,no. I could have you here forever and be happy!"

"For that I am so pleased. Truly I would love it. I have discovered I love the sea -- that is, beside it but not on it!! I wish there were some way I could always be living by it , but...."

"Yes, I know, but you can always come for a visit, you know, and stay as long as you like and THEN you can bring baby!"

"Well now.Down to serious thinking. I am in the middle of my third month. Perhaps....."

"Why don't we `perhaps' in two weeks...?"

"Well, if that won't be outstaying my welcome....

Two weeks would be great. Dan will be settled in Jerusalem then, and maybe those two will get married. Then, of course, Alex can stop the nagging.His notes are dreadfully lonesome."

"All right. We can head for that time. Meanwhile just don't talk about going! I am lonesome already. This visit has been so special."

The next weeks it was all fun and spaced in with shopping, packing and in general getting ready for another trek. Tribune Fabius assigned two Auxiliaries and drivers for the trip because the original Auxiliaries had returned to Philippi.

A driver was assigned because Dan was not at Caesarea and the road was rough and steep. Claudia donated several huge sitting pillows because it was too precarious on the seats themselves, so they were taken out.

About the middle of the third week, the day of departure arrived. Once Jerusalem had been reached and everyone was at a home base, the Auxiliaries and Drivers would return with both wagons. `Tiny" wagon had truly found its mission with the arrival of the Gaius party months ago. Goodbye was a time of weeping and laughing and promises for future visits. Claudia handed up a big bundle to Portia, "You can open this only when you have found home and are ready to plan the nursery. It comes to baby with much love.

A typically feminine gesture with the typically feminine reaction of tears and sad goodbyes.

CHAPTER TWELVE

Portia's letter announcing her pregnancy hit Gaius with terrible impact. His stomach writhed in knots, and he shook with rage. The scribe assigned to him had approached to ask a question, and, as he looked up, he saw that the Tribune's face was diffused with red and white splotches as if he were possibly having a stroke.

"Are you all right, Sir?" The Greek asked tremulously.

Gaius did not hear him. There was a roaring in his ears, and he felt suddenly ill.

The Scribe ran and summoned the guard, and the two of them returned to find Gaius holding onto the table before the courtyard window. With one on either side, they eased him into the great chair before his desk.

"I'll be all right," he murmured. Then seeing the two of them looking at him with genuine concern, he stumbled back to his apartment, turned and ordered:

"Cancel my appointments, and do not disturb me!"

With this, he disappeared into the privacy of his own room.

His first thoughts were of divorce and exposure of Portia for what he saw her to be, a lying whore. And how..with whom..could she have had such secretive sex as to have become pregnant? He recalled that she had shown a vivacious interest in Sinstra, but Sinstra had been with him here in Jerusalem all along. Who then? Cassius was the only remaining choice. Gaius had been gone for weeks, leaving him in charge of the garrison. Plenty of opportunity. But how, in the name of Zeus, could she have ever been interested in a man scarcely older than herself?

As these thoughts tumbled through his mind, he remembered Cassius' growth from a youth to a very muscular young man; and the inexorable comparison with himself was painful. Little wonder, in truth, that she did find him more attractive than this, his own aging and crippled body!

Well, what would he do now? Despite his being the instigator of divorce which seemed so desirable, there still would be snickering in the garrison that it was she who was ditching an old man too old to..well, too old for what? He still enjoyed a woman now and then. But did they enjoy him? He didn't know, and Portia was too naive to judge. Come to think of it, he <u>was</u> too old, or at least too sterile, to ever father a child. But if Portia delivered a child and seemed contentedly happy, who would ever suspect the truth? Ah, there was the rub.

He and Portia..and <u>now</u> the other man, damn him, the three knew the truth. Of course, Portia was still an ignorant child and might never really know that the child was not his. Her letter made no mention of leaving him. So that just left the other man to know, in all likelihood, that he was sterile..that is, if he gave any thought to it at all. And that other man, certainly Cassius, would live his whole lifetime through with the amused satisfaction that he, the old man, would have to raise his child! The final thought (the convulsing thought bent him double)..like as not, given the opportunity, Portia and Cassius would resume where they left off!

The arrangement would leak out slowly at first, and then everyone would know; and he would be the laughingstock of the whole Command!

Wiping the sweat from his face, The Tribune saw clearly what must be done. Cassius must be disposed of with no fanfare, just be quietly missing from the scene. Some silly person might call it murder, but labels at a time like this were of little concern. As in all of the battles that he had fought, it was understood that some must be destroyed for the good of others..in this case, Romans.

Oddly enough, the consideration calmed him, and the pain lessened. He opened his door and ordered that cold milk be sent. The task was before him..the method as yet not certain. He no longer dare think of Cassius as his son. Gaius should have known that the damned Greek could never be a true Roman! Some things were just not meant to be.

Portia was glad neither she nor Lea had to drive, for the Tribune had surely been right..the road was rough and up ahead even she could see how it climbed. With the swaying of the wagon both Petta and Lea fell asleep. Portia was too concerned with the future and her mind darted ahead to Gaius and their meeting. Reaching inside the little leather jerkin she was wearing, Portia took out Gaius' letter replying to hers which Dr. Tibius had delivered.

He had written two little notes to her in Caesarea, but this one deserved a lot of study. The tone of it wasn't much like what she would have expected. Had Lea seen her she would have been disturbed, for Portia's expression was one of puzzled concern.

'My dear Wife,' it began...so formal. She shrugged and went on.

"The Doctor delivered your diagnosis in your own handwriting, and he confirmed what you said. How overjoyed you must be with the thought of a baby! I am happy for you and hope that this is all you expect it to be. Never expecting myself to play the role of a father, I am not sure how to look forward to this venture. I shall do my best for you and the child, always. Let me know when you will be coming to Jerusalem so that I can arrange proper housing. Love, Alexander."

Staring into space her thoughts searched for a reason for the tone of this letter, which she had, however foolishly, expected to be received happily. There was no joy, no outward displeasure. Just not much. It was, if anything, impersonal and business-like. Why? What was he thinking? What had happened in Jerusalem back then when she wrote the letter, to take him so far away from the Alexander that she knew? Even the little notes received at Claudia's were friendlier..not much, but some. Could it be that Alex suspected that the baby was not his?

The wheels of the wagon taking her closer and closer to Jerusalem, clicked with disturbing monotony, strangely like the letter.

CHAPTER THIRTEEN

Jesus stood on the small flat portion of rocky soil that made up his makeshift podium. His arms were folded, and he looked down serenely on the milling crowd before him. The whimpers and cries of children here and there wafted into the air. Cassius waited quietly on his perch behind the podium and wondered why it was that he felt a tingle of excitement. Then, Jesus raised his arms with his palms extended toward those before him:

"You are the Salt of The Earth!"' his rich baritone rolled over the crowd. "But," he paused dramatically, "if the salt loses its flavor, how shall it be flavored? You are the light of the world. A city set on a hill cannot be hidden.(1)

"*This* rabble is the "salt of the earth"? went through Cassius' mind. `Light of The World'? What does Jesus see that I don't?"

But the morning went as if time were not in it. The sun was setting behind the hills and casting long shadows when Jesus turned and walked back among the boulders which had become his only sanctuary.

"Have you seen enough..`listened and learned' as you say?" Simon asked.

They were eating some of the delicious trout that seemed to abound in the stream behind them. Cassius felt ravenously hungry but so excited that he scarcely tasted the food.

"What did he mean about the angels rejoicing over the repenting of one sinner? What does he mean..`repent', and what is a `sinner'?"

Simon gazed at him in wonderment.

"You really are a Roman, aren't you..truly an ignorant Gentile?"

Cassius bristled.

"I am not ignorant, Simon. But I do not understand what Jesus is all about."

"Then, I ask, are you familiar with the Torah?"

(1) New Testament, Gospel of Matthew, Ch.5.

"No."

"Thousands of years ago, Abram was chosen by God..that's our God, Yahweh..he was chosen to be the father of our nation, the beginning, if you will, of a people..his people. Years later, he chose Moses to lead our people out of captivity in Egypt; and he gave to him the Ten Commandments by which we live. He, Yahweh, talked with Moses and inspired him to write the five great books which make up the Torah."

"So what has this to do with Jesus?"

"Well, we have been a proud people, proud and, I'm sorry to say, arrogant. We have been hated by the Philistines whose land this was before God gave it to us, and we have been hated through all the years since...hated, persecuted, conquered, and scattered to the four corners of the Earth."

"Yes, I have known some of this. But again, what has this to do with Jesus?"

"Among our people, during these many years, we have had what we call `prophets', men and women whom God has chosen to give additional knowledge. Many of them, most notably Isaiah who lived about seven hundred years ago, have foretold that one day, a man would be born who would deliver us from the bondage of conquerors and be our king forever. Jesus is that man."

"But where is his army? And how could he ever be a king? He doesn't even mention anything of being a king. As you and I have seen, every kind of person has gathered here, though I don't know for what reason. And Jesus seems to be concerned with this repentance thing. I don't get it!"

Simon chuckled.

"No, I don't suppose that you would. But I have a very strong feeling that you will, you will. Meanwhile, good night, Elias of Siracusa."

How could Simon go to sleep so quickly and leave him so completely baffled was a mystery in itself. Time was passing by, and he knew so little. Why would Gaius so utterly misunderstand this whole thing? Of course, if Jesus did plan to be king..but the idea was absurd. Still, if these people living out here in the desert for days on end were any indication of his popularity, maybe that was what had Pontius Pilate worried.

And yet once again, a very perplexed Cassius slept under the stars.

Cassius awakened with Simon standing over him, and, while the sleeper gave no evidence of waking, he studied the perplexed face of the disciple.

"Why are you so concerned, Simon?"

Cassius smiled.

Surprised and a little disgusted with having been found out, Simon grunted and turned to walk to the fire.

"Our breakfast is waiting to be eaten," he said.

When they were well into the meal, he sat back and said reflectively:

"You know, when I befriended you, I had no idea that I would become nursemaid to a Roman."

Cassius grinned.

"You could have done worse.." Then he added:

"I really do appreciate your kindness or friendship or just watching over me to protect Jesus..I really don't care. You have really helped."

"How have I helped you? I don't truly know what you're doing here."

"And I can't tell you..at least, not yet. Has Jesus asked any questions about me? Sitting up there in my niche, I have been rather conspicuous."

"No, he has not asked any questions, though he knows that you're here. I think that he's just busy with his ministry, much too busy to bother with a fake Jew."

Cassius ignored the gig.

"You know by now that I have no intent to harm him. Tell me, Simon, when does he plan to take over the Throne of David?"

"From what I can see, never. We have hoped for three years that he would fulfill the prophecy; but, instead, he thinks he will die on a cross."

"But why? He has not committed any crimes that I know of.~

113

"Not even Jesus can insult the Pharisees and Sadducees continually and get away with it. He is destroying the power that they had since the days of Moses, and even here in the wilderness, they spy on him and criticize him for dining with sinners."

"What `sinners'?"

"You saw that group of Publicans, your tax-collectors, that came out last week, and that other bunch of riff-raff from Greece..these are the despicable `sinners' that they're talking about. And Jesus did eat with them and answer their questions."

Cassius continued to eat the fresh fruit before him.

"How important is all of this? I have been feeling uneasy when Jesus talks. I don't know why this thing of sinners is so important to him; but that and repentance seems to be everything to him." Then, for a moment, a peach seed required his attention; and when that was dug out, he asked:

"What of a girl-friend or wife? Doesn't he ever go home?"

Simon was apparently surprised with the question.

"Elias, the Son of God..Jesus as you see him..has neither home nor wife. For that matter, none of us who have been with him for so many months now..none of us have any life at all except to be with him." For the first time, his features softened.

"This, then, is that important to you?" Cassius asked.

"It is life itself, my heathen friend."

Then, as if he might have said too much, Simon busied himself with sweeping the dust from his bed covering and began to put his few utensils together for transport.

"You are leaving?"

Simon stopped and looked at Cassius.

"Haven't you seen enough to know about Jesus?"

"If you are suggesting that I stay here, no..I will not. Where are you going?"

Simon sighed with disgust.

"If you must know, we are going to Bethany. A dear friend of Jesus, Lazarus by name, is ill. No doubt, Jesus will heal him."

Cassius considered his situation. The crowd had already begun to disperse with some going South and others North.

"On second thought, Simon, I believe that I *will* stay here for a while. These fish are too good to leave behind."

Simon studied him for a long moment, wondering just why Cassius had so quickly changed his mind.

"Hmm..I see. Well, peace to you, Elias of Siracusa, or whoever you are. I thought..oh well, Shalom."

The disciples and Jesus were soon out of sight, walking with steady gait to the West. Cassius knew that they would go as far as Jericho and then turn South toward Bethany. He knew that they would have to camp somewhere along the way, and he would catch up quietly so that no one would know that he had followed them. In a new locale, around different people, Jesus might well divulge more of his plans than the past few days of February had revealed.

Horse seemed to cherish his company. He wiggled his ears and muzzled for a bite of apple to vary his usual diet of oats and wheat.

"So you too are lonely, you homely brute? Well, so am I. Let's get out of here!"

Cassius pitched his bedding and few remaining food supplies onto the beast, and they headed West in the direction taken by the disciples. Cassius pulled Horse into a steady trot to which he objected, but he had no choice but to follow. The exercise was refreshing to Cassius, and he was glad for the opportunity to jog.

Meanwhile and far ahead, the craggy fisherman watched him from atop a ledge of the mountain path. Simon smiled.

"All is well, I haven't lost him after all"

The Centurion and his burro slowed to a fast walk, moving steadily toward the Jordan River. They paused only to eat at noon and to drink sparingly, but they still had not caught up with the disciples as the Sun began to set, casting long shadows across the stark hills. Cassius remembered that a full moon had lit the sky last night, and with there being no clouds, he should have no trouble continuing to travel after sunset if need be.

Presently they crossed the Jordan, pausing long enough for Horse to drink deeply and then for both of them to enjoy a meal and rest. They still might have to sprint to catch up.

The figs bought in Capernaum were almost gone, and he was glad that he was finishing the last of the trout. Jericho would surely provide ample opportunity to restock his food supply, and hopefully, he could also buy some freshly baked bread and cakes. He lay back against his folded cloak and watched lazily as the stars began to appear in the evening sky. He was thinking of Portia and remembering her soft, sensuous lips when the peace of the evening was shattered with Horse's bray..a long reverberating blast of sound which echoed off the canyon walls and cascaded into the night.

"Stupid animal!" he barked. "Shut up! Do you want to tell everyone that we're here?" Horse was not impressed and brayed into the second verse of whatever song he imagined himself to be singing.

"Peace, My Friend, peace," Simon said as he walked into the circle of light of the fire. "Your animal is just lonely as I suspect that we all are."

He looked around the camp.

"I see that you've eaten. So have we. We're just a bit further down the trail. I have been expecting you."

Cassius looked at him, surprised and a little chagrined to realize that he had failed utterly in affecting an unannounced arrival.

"Yes, Elias. I have known since yesterday that you would be here, though I didn't quite understand your wish to be secretive."

Cassius replied:

"I have no wish to be `secretive', as you put it; I just think that Jesus might express himself differently if he thought me not to be in his audience."

Simon laughed at his naivete.

"We have nothing to burden us this evening, no crowd to consider; and that gives a chance to ask you..what did you mean when you said that you felt `uneasy' when Jesus was talking?~

Cassius stared quietly into the embers of the fire.

" I don't know just how to express it. Jesus has spoken in one way or another, usually in those little stories that he makes up, but he has talked of something he calls `sin'." He stopped as if thinking, and Simon wisely said nothing..just waiting.

"I think it must be something like that which bothers me. Do you understand?"

116

"No."

"I have done a bad thing. I am deeply in love. Neither of us planned it that way. It just happened. The other man is my senior officer, a man older than I by many years and just as much older than his wife. I am miserable, and so is she. I wish that it had never happened in a way; and yet, nothing in life ever meant so much to either of us. Is this sin, Simon?"

Simon answered quietly, hoping that at long last, he could know why this strange young man followed so persistently and still avoided Jesus.

"Oh, yes, my young friend. This is a sin, an affront in any society, often punishable by death. But it has happened. What are you planning to do about it?"

"I wish I knew. I am miserable when I sleep and when I wake. Peculiarly, the only time that I ever feel any sense of peace at all is when Jesus is talking..and he isn't even talking to me."

"Oh, yes," Simon replied," he *is* talking to you just as much as he ever talked to anyone. You have said that you do not wish to talk with Jesus, but you are telling me about it. Would you like to do the right thing?"

"Is there a `right thing'?"

Simon realized suddenly that he just might be in over his head. He looked off into the night.

"Possibly there is, I suppose. There just might be." Then he looked back at Cassius.

"But I don't even know who you really are and what you're doing here. And I can't help unless I do."

"All right. You shall know." Cassius paused to sip some water.

~I was the son of a Greek slave in the home of a Roman Senator. My name was Dismas. The Senator's son died, and so, because I was of the son's age, I became like a son to him. The old man never got around to adopting me legally before he died, but he did ask his closest friend, a Tribune, to take care of me. He did. He gave me the old man's name; and, with the rights of Imperium of his office, he made me a Centurion. This is the wonderful man that I have betrayed."

"So your name now is..?"

"Centurion Cassius Voltanus."

Simon sat back for a moment as if to take it all in.

"So now, I understand all of that. But I still don't know why you're here."

"Pontius Pilate, perhaps Tiberius himself for all I know, well, they're worried about Jesus. They think that he may be planning to overthrow the Roman government in Palestine. It's up to me to report back on what I see and hear."

"You have been with me for weeks. You have heard Jesus and seen what he does. How would you describe him now?"

"So far as I can tell, he hurts no one, and he hates no one except, perhaps, those Jews called Pharisees. He has been said to be the Son of God, whoever that is, but he is not like anyone I have ever known before. One does not love men, but I think that I could love him if.."

"If what?"`

"If only he could know all about me and forgive me for what I have to do."

Simon was deeply moved. He walked away from the glow of the fire, and Cassius saw him hold up his arms toward the sky. He stood there silently for quite a while, and then he returned.

"You have sinned greatly, Cassius Voltanus. Would you like to be free of this sin?"

"Oh, yes, if I could..but how?"

"Follow me."

Simon turned and walked back toward the river. Cassius followed.

"Now, take off all of your clothes except your underwear."

"Why?"

"You have confessed your sins to me; and though you have never talked with Jesus, I assure you that He knows all about you. If you wish, I will baptize you here; and your sins..all of them..will be forgiven. Jesus will know, and the angels of Heaven will rejoice!"

Simon took Cassius by the hand, laid him back into the flowing stream, and lifted him back up again. Inexplicably, despite the cold water, Cassius felt a warm glow and a great joy.

All was right in his life again!

Simon's voice cut into his thoughts:

"There is so much that you must know, though I myself do not know why. This is not the time to begin to tell you now; and so, tomorrow when Jesus is talking, you and I will meet here."

Simon chuckled then, and addressing himself, asked:

"What is this that I have come to..teaching a Greek, or worse yet..a Roman?" Then he close his eyes and murmured softly: "But Your will be done. I will not question it."

Leaving Cassius in bewilderment, he walked off into the night.

Cassius slept little. Caught up in a strange excitement, and trying to salvage some sense of reality, he found that sleep was out of the question. Then, as light began to dawn again in the East, he slept in sheer exhaustion.

The smell of lamb roasting over the fire served as his wake-up call. He was as pleased to see Simon already waiting for him as he was hungry for food.

"So! My learner awakes! Come join me, Centurion Voltanus. Without food, you can't learn. And if you don't learn, you too will pass and your place remembered no more. But enough of this. I have fed your burro, washed your fruit, and wait now for you to do your part..eat. and be a man!"

Both laughed, and Cassius ate as if his life had just begun.

Only a short time later, the two of them sat in the shade of a tree beside the Jordan.

Simon said:

"You may recall that our people, our whole Jewish race, began with a man named Abram. Since then, God has led us through the leadership of such great men as Moses and taught us with prophets like Elijah, Isaiah, and especially, Daniel. Through him, Mighty Centurion, you will learn that Rome is not forever. Shall we begin?"

Thus it was that the fisherman-turned-teacher and the soldier spent the day while the forces of decay were at work on Lazarus. It was his fourth day in the tomb.

CHAPTER FOURTEEN

Portia, and Petta in their comfy cushion-seats were fascinated with the rolling, rugged, and rocky beauty of the land as the wagon climbed up, across and around on the road leading to Jerusalem, situated some 2600 feet above sea level on its own domain of low, rolling hills. Lea, sitting up beside the driver, was equally intrigued. There were trees scattered indiscriminately but no profusion of greenery such as was found near the Jordan or on the cultivated terraces.

Most of the way from Caesarea, they had traveled the level, worn roads near the sea, roads frequented heavily with foot travelers up and down the land. Now, to reach Jerusalem, there were the rolling hills, and valleys -- a challenge to all travelers. Rounding a bend in the road, Portia gasped,

"Oh, look! Is that Jerusalem?" her eyes were riveted on a wall above them, still a good climb away.

"Yes, Ma'am. We shall be able to see it more clearly in just a bit now. It stretches all across those hills and is truly quite a site -- you'll see."

And, indeed, it was. When they could see the panorama of the city above them, surrounded by the wall, it appeared to set upon its own platform with a road climbing to enter a huge gate. The earth around the wall looked rather like a shallow cliff with cultivated terraces and orchards at the base. The road they were now traveling was the main route from Galilee; and even from here, Portia could see the top of the four towers of the Fortress of Antonia as well as the towering height of the Temple.

Her voice was filled with awe and wonder, as she spoke:

"The whole place glows...like...well, like there was light within the stone! What is it?"

"It is just the stone. Perhaps it is the kind of stone. I don't know, Ma'am. I know that Jerusalem is the only place that looks like this. It is sort of special, isn't it?" The driver seemed equally impressed despite the fact he had seen it all many times.

The two Auxiliaries moved their mounts to flank the passenger wagon which led the way, and the driver of the cargo wagon closed up the space between his team and the rear of the little wagon as they entered the huge gate. The women were wide-eyed with wonder looking up at the imposing gate towers. The tiny group moved swiftly forward on a fairly wide road toward the Fortress and made a wide turn to the right to come to a stop below and in front of the ascending stairway between two of the huge towers. One Auxiliary dismounted and went up the steps on the double, to disappear through an arched entry.

People looked at the little group with interest as they passed by; but, interestingly enough, the arrival of the traveling group did not seem to be anything out of the ordinary to those within the city which was a busy bustling place in its own right. The girls' eyes, however, were wide and staring. The place was so different from Philippi and not at all like Rome.

They waited a short time for the Auxiliary to return. When he did, the driver of the little wagon followed his directions to move back the way they had come and then circle the first tower to proceed to an entry with a gate on the far side of the Fortress wall.

Entering they found themselves inside a large military enclosure. From somewhere Gaius appeared. His office was apparently one of many built into the wide Fortress wall, through which they had just entered. When they saw Gaius approach, Lea and Petta quickly got out of the wagon and waited as Tribune Gaius helped Portia to the ground. Alex and Portia embraced one another.

"How good to see you, Alex! You do look rested! I must be a wreck!"

"You look mighty good to me, my girl...a little plump, of course!" He smiled, and all three of the women giggled.

"Now, let's get you organized. Gather out of the big wagon all you might need for a few days, and put it with the things you have bundled back there...." he gestured to their travel bundles, then continued,

"My quarters have been here at the Antonia, but I have located a small place for us and I will give the driver directions to take you there. We'll keep the big wagon here for a day or so, until we get really organized. When you get to the house, settle in as best you can. I will arrive in a couple of hours with my belongings as well as our dinner -- all cooked! How does that sound?"

"Wonderful!"

"Good. Up you go again."

"I will be happy, indeed, to uncurl and stretch!!"

When they were all back in the wagon, with a few more of their necessities stored away in the back of the wagon, the driver took up the reins. Alex waved them off and the little wagon re-entered the traffic outside the Fortress walls. The driver was familiar with the city and easily followed the directions given him by Tribune Gaius. They did not have far to go because the little house the Tribune had chosen was within the living area near the Fortress, quite close to the wall in a section that had gardens and a view of the Mount of Olives. Portia was thrilled as they pulled into the courtyard of the little place. It was so clean and shining. A fountain gurgled a welcome from the center of the courtyard.

Inside, the place was perfect in size with generous Master quarters, a good kitchen and dining area with an all purpose room. To the rear, near the kitchen, were several small rooms for servants and, even, a small all- purpose room for them.

In the back, their garden ran from the house to the big wall, and it was full of growing things. Everyone excitedly set about bringing in their belongings. Each room had its own furniture and it was all very nice indeed.

The Tribune arrived as promised and with the help of the driver who had awaited his arrival, carried in the food he had brought. There was lamb, fowl, roasted potatoes and a basket of fresh vegetables and fruit and some special cakes -- a veritable feast!

"There's so much, Alex! But it surely does have a tantalizing fragrance!"

"There is a cold-closet here, too...so Petta will have time to get acquainted with her cooking room and still feed us without first having to hang over a hot stove!"

"Oh, thank you, Tribune!" Petta bowed graciously.

Lea helped Petta set forth the dishes for the Tribune and Portia in the dining area, and plates for themselves on a little table in the kitchen while Alex and Portia carried his belongings into the Master Quarters.

Very shortly everyone had served themselves from the bounty set forth on the big counter in the cooking room. In the dining area a large window overlooked the garden which was now shadowed with approaching evening.

"Oh, Alex...it is such a lovely little house, and so very quiet. And, how peaceful the garden is!"

"I am glad you like it, my Dear."

Portia was strangely uncomfortable, despite the lovely little house, the peaceful garden, and Alex' graciousness in having thought of all the necessities of arrival. What was it? Covertly she studied his face. Same face, but different. Just very military! That was about all that came to mind. Come to think of it, he had not looked at her directly since her arrival!! Perhaps he was very preoccupied? Perhaps he was just tired, as was she...that was it -tired. She put it down until they had chance to be alone and relax.

"How are you feeling, Portia?"

His voice startled her reverie.

"Oh..Oh, quite well now. The rest at Caesarea with Claudia helped so much. I - I didn't know what was wrong for so long...but when I knew there was nothing really wrong, I felt better right away. Are...are you pleased, Alex? You have said almost nothing."

"Pleased? I - I can't really say...I must get used to the idea first. It just isn't anything I know about, you know..."

Inexplicably she burst into laughter and he looked at her in astonishment. Still giggling, she blurted:

"It's just not military strategy, is it?"

"No, it is not. You are quite right!"

In spite of himself, he laughed - just briefly, and she joined in. It was a relieving break through. They each felt better, he in spite of himself. She in gratitude that her sense of humor had saved them, for now anyway.

Quite suddenly fatigue caught up with her. She could feel herself literally wilting.

"Alex, I am so tired. I just realized I must get to bed without delay. Forgive me, will you?

"Of course. I'll be with you, very soon. Go along."

"Goodnight, Alex. Thank you for everything."

When she awoke, a good ten hours later, she felt wonderful. How quiet it was, wonderful and so restful. Alex' side of the bed was rumpled so he had been there, though he was gone now. She realized she was grateful for that. She pondered this reaction, staring at the ceiling. The moment she had laid eyes on him at the Fortress, she knew something was awry. Now she was sure of it and equally puzzled with her own reaction. Across the miles and down the road of time she could hear her Father's voice in counsel,

"Portia, remember this always. If you don't understand something or someone, have the wisdom to keep quiet. Words can be wicked tools unless used wisely. In silence there is more than quiet...there is often salvation."

"Thank you, Papa," she said. She blew him a kiss, clear from Jerusalem. Then, she rose, in peace of mind, and set about the new day in a new world.

It really took a week for Portia to feel rested and "in place" so to speak in this new house and the new world in which she found herself. Lea had been so lucky - because of Dan, naturally. He had known of the little house before they arrived and then watched for them. Coming to welcome them the very next day after their arrival, had sealed his relationship with Lea. They were to be married in about a month or so. Lea would spend her days with Portia while Dan established his own working situation, so there was no change to be faced in that regard.

After the first week and feeling more rested and, too, excited with the movement of the child within her, Portia began to face life in Jerusalem with a very different Alex. There was no `ease' within him, it seemed. Though she did not understand it she said nothing and just chattered on at his stern countenance and patiently bore the `military' manner. Alex was thoroughly absorbed with whatever he was involved with here at the

Antonia and so, of course, she just dismissed him from her thinking for the most part, wondering about Cassius. Would she see him and if so, would she be able to contain herself within the role she must play? These thoughts, which she had forbidden herself, upset her and so she pushed them away and concentrated on getting things ready for the baby. There were about three more months to wait for the child.

The second week of her residence everything changed with Alex' sudden exhibition of agitation. One day he was as when she had arrived and the next the agitation claimed him and he rushed from the house early to meet with Pilate, the Governor.

For two days following that meeting, he paced the floor when he was home, ate little and always rushed to his office. She watched as Alex paled and suddenly began to turn old before her eyes. She tried to make him rest but he shoved her aside with :

"Rest! I dare not rest!"

She too became silent, depressed with what she did not understand. Even the child's movements were less violent - hardly noticed. Finally, on the third day after that meeting of the week, Gaius - gray faced and distracted, turned to her before leaving the house.

"Thank you, Portia, for just being you. Things are not going well, and just knowing you are here is what gives me strength. I am a lucky man. Good day..."

She would have spoken but his raised hand stilled her response. That and the gray, splotchy color of his skin.

"I'll see you at dinner." were his words, and he left the house. She speechlessly had watched him go, distressed that he did not act like her familiar Alex or, even, look like him. There seemed nothing she could turn her mind to. Even relaxing was disturbing. As usual she sought the courtyard with the friendly fountain. All her life the bubbling of streams in Alba had warmed her spirit and everywhere she had lived with Alex there had been a bubbling fountain to quiet her mind and emotions.

Sitting on the edge of the fountain, her fingers dabbling in the water quieted her and her mind felt `smoothed'. That was the word that came to her mind as she realized the distress had lessened. She silently thought of the word smooth and her mind took her to the sea, like where Claudia was..or..or,of course, Alba -- home! She was suddenly so homesick she wanted to cry. And all at once she knew that home was not Rome -- never had been, and Jerusalem never could be. She sat there for some time until the homesickness subsided with the sudden kicking inside her belly and from that she was filled with joy and went into the house and up to her room where she again worked with the baby clothes.

CHAPTER FIFTEEN

In the peculiar arrangement of being part of the group and yet ostensibly an independent traveler, Cassius continued to walk just outside the Jesus group. The situation seemed ridiculous on the face of it, for Simon must surely have had to answer questions about Cassius' continued presence. Still, there was a job to do, and he was doing it.

On this, the fourth day of traveling since they had left Gadara, they began their descent into the outskirts of the village of Bethany. They had just entered an area in which the homes seemed to be larger and in better repair than others around them when a very pretty girl suddenly broke through a group in her front yard and ran to greet Jesus. As Cassius drew nearer, he saw that she was crying; and, in a tone that was almost accusatory, she said:

"He would not have died if you had been here."

As if he were somehow amiss in not having come sooner, Jesus replied:

"Your brother will rise again." (1)

He had continued to move toward the village so as not to appear to be with Jesus but to be close enough to observe his actions. Fortunately, Jesus' voice carried over the other sounds, and Cassius heard him say:

"I am the Resurrection and the Life. He who believes in me, though he may die, he shall live. And whoever lives and believes in me shall never die."

Now peering intently at the young woman, he asked:

"Do you believe this?"

Her reply, whatever it was, ended abruptly, and she ran back into the house to get another woman, slightly older than herself. She ran to Jesus and fell at his feet. She too said:

"Lord, if you had been here, my brother would not have died."

(1) New Testament, Gospel of John, Ch. 11, vss.20-43.

So, the two women were obviously sisters. But what did they expect of Jesus?

The sobbing between the two sisters resumed, and the number of people who had gathered around them also wept. As Jesus embraced the two, tears glistened on his own cheeks, and he asked:

"Where have you laid him?"

The group then began moving down a path which happened to be where Cassius was standing, and so he moved along in front until they reached a cave which was blocked with a large stone.

"Remove the stone," Jesus commanded.

"But, Lord, by this time, there will be a stench, for Lazarus has been dead four days."

Cassius recalled all too well the smell of the rotting flesh of men and horses on the battlefields. However, partly from curiosity and partly from the practical necessity of appearing to be one of the group, he stepped forward and rolled back the stone. The air in the cave seemed strangely fresh. The only smell was that of the sweetness of the cloves used to embalm Lazarus.

As Cassius looked, he saw that Jesus had lifted his arms, apparently in prayer. He turned and pointed directly at the tomb. Calling loudly, he said:

"Lazarus, come forth!"

As the crowd watched incredulously, a figure appeared in the open mouth of the cave. He was still bound hand and foot but bobbed his head vigorously toward Jesus.

"Loose him, and let him go!"

As Cassius' knife deftly cut away the bonds, the two sisters surged forward and held a bewildered Lazarus in delirious embrace.

Cassius knew that all eyes would be on Lazarus and Jesus, so that he could again slip into the back of the crowd. He had just picked up Horse's reins again when he felt detained. As he looked back for only the briefest moment, he found himself looking directly into the eyes of Jesus.

As never in all of his life, he felt drenched in love. He felt an incredible heat, and he couldn't move.   Jesus' expression said it all so plainly..understanding, forgiveness, and an almost melancholy sadness. Then he smiled slightly and reached to embrace the risen Lazarus.

Bethany was only two miles from Jerusalem, and Cassius entertained the thought that his assignment might be finished. With Passover being just a few weeks away, he had assumed that Jesus would wish to be in Jerusalem just to rest if nothing else. But to his disappointment, Simon pointed out some in the crowd who were apparently focused on Jesus' actions, as if he were going to perform some sort of legerdemain.

"Those are going to watch to find fault. They will be with us in every walk we make, intent always in finding fault with The Master.   This miracle of raising Lazarus for most of us was indeed absolutely certain proof that Jesus is the Son of God. But for them, this miracle was of no moment except to undermine further the hold that the Pharisees have on the people. Raising Lazarus was the last straw. There is no way that it could have been faked, and so the die is cast."

Simon had never been so talkative.still what could he mean?

"What I mean-said plainly-is that these hyenas are waiting to kill Jesus."

"Well, we are only two miles from Jerusalem. What can we do to save him?"

Simon smiled.

"Isn't it interesting that you are concerned now with `saving him'?"

"Could I be otherwise, though, of course, I'll have to present an objective report.."

And then the Centurion laughed. "How can you tell of the miracles of Jesus and be objective?"

The pleasantries of the visit were abruptly cut short. Visits with the two sisters and their still somewhat bewildered brother were cut short, and once again the Jesus group was on the move. Surprisingly, they walked North, clearly toward Jerusalem itself. But instead of choosing the upward road leading into the city, they continued to yet another division of the road which led into the wilderness of Samaria.   Continuing North and West, they traveled along the road which followed along the foothills. As the Sun was setting and both Horse and Cassius were wondering where they would spend the night, they came to the village of Ephraim. The goats were being milked and the children gathered for the night. Cassius looked on wistfully and wondered whether he and Portia would ever have the joy of gathering their children at dusk and settling at days end in that wonderful place called "home".

His supplies were running short, and he was low on grain for Horse. The scurrying out to this hamlet of Samaria had been nothing short of escape, because he knew that soldiers of the Sanhedrin would have been directed tomorrow to seize Jesus if they could find him in Bethany.

He had just dipped deeply into the remaining grain for his burro when he saw a movement at the edge of his campsite. It was not Simon, nor was it any other of the apostles. So as not to show that he knew of the stranger's presence, Cassius continued to prepare for the night. The stranger edged forward hesitantly and then addressed him in Aramaic:

"You are with Jesus?" he asked.

Cassius looked him over, a slight man dressed in the plainness of the desert people.

"Yes. I am with Jesus. Why do you ask?"

"I have meat prepared for you as with the others. And there is fruit also grown here on our land. You have blessed us with your coming. Peace be to you." And as Cassius watched in delighted surprise, the unnamed Samaritan put down the container of roast lamb and two gorgeous peaches. And then he was gone, quietly as he had come.

The desert country around Ephraim was barren and desolate. It was a natural choice for a leper colony; and there, perhaps just a mile or so out of town, some of the fetid caste-offs of society were gathered to deteriorate and die. Death had been slowed for some of the men; and in their vestigial state, ten were in almost constant touch to commiserate or to lend patient ears to stories oft-repeated of life on the outside. It was to this strange group that the word came..Jesus would pass along the main road tomorrow. The word was passed among them quietly. In the

132

still of the night while the guards kept careless watch, one by one they slipped up the small canyon shielded from the view of the guards. The desert night was cruel as its days warmth fled into the air mass, and the temperature approached freezing. The ten men huddled closely together with their teeth chattering in the narrow canyon leading to the main road of commerce. But they had no choice, for a fire would have revealed their escape.

The long rays of the rising sun came at long last and with them, the cheering warmth of the day.

"They're coming, they're coming!" exclaimed one of the men hoarsely. The Jesus group had eaten early, devoted perhaps an hour to prayer, and was now walking along the well-traveled road toward one of the few oasis of the Samaritan desert. Cassius was, as usual, traveling well to the rear of the main group; and it was he who first detected the smell of rotting flesh now blowing down-wind from the lepers. As Jesus and the others made the turn of the road, the lepers called out to him:

"Jesus, have mercy on us..have mercy..have mercy!"

Jesus stopped and looked at the desperate men.

"I wonder what they think he can do out here," Cassius mused. Perhaps the same thought went through Jesus' mind. At any rate, he lifted his hand to point toward them and said:

"Go! Show yourselves to the priests." (1)

The lepers stopped calling and said nothing more. Purposefully, they walked down the road from Jesus had come, their obvious intent being to go Ephraim and there, to show themselves as Jesus had said.

What a dangerous order..indeed, what a calamitous situation if, having been ordered to keep their distance, they appeared instead among the faithful at the synagogue! Well, perhaps the desperate circumstance justified a dangerous act.

The thoughts slipped from his mind, and Cassius followed the disciples a short distance farther to an area of palm trees and fresh, clear water which bubbled from a spring and formed a welcome pool for men and animals alike to drink, bathe, and be refreshed. Obviously, this was the objective in their walking into

(1) Luke: 17

the desert; because it was here that caravans were in constant transition. What better place could Jesus have chosen to preach his message?

Horse was lead to the lower end of the pool and drank deeply. Cassius welcomed the chance to refill his canteen and to wash his tired dirty feet in cold water. Cleansed and relaxed, he had almost fallen asleep in the shade of a palm tree when the quiet of the late afternoon was shattered with the cries of a man approaching the oasis on a dead run and leaping to shout as he ran.

"Master, master!" he called. And then as he ran by, Cassius realized that the filthy, blood-stained rags on the man were those of one of the ten lepers of the early morning. He fell head-long at the feet of Jesus, sobbing with the joy of one restored to life again. The sores, the pitted tissues of his arms, and the ravaged features of his face..all now were whole again. Only the whiteness of the new flesh indicated his previous condition.

"But were there not ten of you..where are the other nine? Has only this foreigner returned to give God the glory?" Then Jesus lifted the man to his feet and urged him to continue his walk to freedom.

The time grew now to only a few weeks before Passover, and nothing more could be gained with staying with the disciples. Jesus' mission was clearly nothing more or less than exhortation to righteousness. If he had any aspirations to ascending the Throne of David, he never mentioned it.

Simon alone watched his preparation to leave as light bathed the oasis on the following morning. Believing it wise to leave as he had come, unannounced, Cassius led Horse back down the road toward Jerusalem.

He had never been to the city, but the Antonia Praetorium was identified easily as he made his way. Horse seemed as eager as he to gain access and comfort from their journey.

As he approached the entrance to the Praetorium, a sturdy young Roman thrust his spear across Cassius' path.

"I am Centurion Cassius Voltanus of the staff of Tribune Alexander Gaius, and I have been assigned to duty here. Summon your Captain of The Guard."

The soldier did not move.

"My orders are to protect our personnel here, Centurion. May I ask the nature of your business here?"

"You may not. You have an order. Do it!"

The young Auxiliary blanched under his helmet and started to answer when the Captain of The Guard emerged from the gate-house. Seeing the luxuriant black beard and long curly hair touching Cassius' shoulders, he bristled:

"You have been denied entrance, Jew. Would you like a bit more of our Roman persuasion?"

Cassius extended the scroll containing his orders.

"I am Centurion Cassius Voltanus of the staff of Tribune Alexander Gaius now resident here. I require the immediate assistance of a stable hand for my burro, the services of a barber, and further, you will dispatch a courier to Tribune Gaius to advise him that I have arrived. Is that clear?"

The Senior Auxiliary gazed in astonishment at the scroll, saluted smartly, and returned his orders.

"Yes, Centurion! My apologies, Sir. We have been on a heightened alert here in Jerusalem with the coming of the Jewish Passover, and we were not expecting you."

Turning briskly, he summoned one man to take Horse, another to escort Cassius to his quarters, and a third to fetch a barber for this strange-looking Roman Officer.

"Your arrival will be announced to the Tribune as soon as possible. Welcome to Antonia, Sir!"

Suddenly, Cassius felt very tired. He was embarrassingly dirty, he smelled bad, and he was weary of the weeks in the wilderness. He had scarcely put his pack down when the barber knocked at the door. Shortly thereafter, black hair littered the floor, and a trim..though decidedly thinner..Centurion Voltanus emerged.

"Oh, how I'm going to enjoy this bath," he exulted as he entered the steam room; and when that was followed by a cleansing bath, he looked forward to hours of sleep on a clean bed. But that delicious experience would have to wait.

"Centurion Voltanus? I am here to escort you to the offices of Tribune Gaius. He has asked that you come as soon as possible."

"Wait there. I'll join you as soon as I have dressed."

He took out his uniform from his pack, did his best to smooth out the wrinkles, and slipped into it. Though he had little time for noticing the little things, it dawned on him that his uniform was almost a sloppy fit. Weeks with little food had taken off the pounds.

He marched vigorously with his Auxiliary escort, though he felt utterly weary. Having mounted the last bank of steps, he stood before massive mahogany doors on which a large replica of the Great Seal of Rome was emblazoned in gold. Two sentries snapped to attention and saluted as his escort opened the doors.

Cassius marched in, wondering all the while just why his presence had been demanded so quickly and why his reception had been staged in such splendor. The gold carpet on which he was standing divided and spread to the right and to the left, forming a border before a slightly raised dias. Two elegant desks were so positioned as to face him. Sitting to his right in full military regalia was Tribune Gaius, while to his left, a small, dark-complexioned man dressed in an impressive gold and black toga, lounged back comfortably in his great chair.

"Stand easy, Centurion," Gaius ordered. Then turning deferentially to the other man, he said:

"This is Centurion Cassius Voltanus, Your Excellency. He is the man that I sent into the Jesus Camp disguised as a Jew; and, from what the guard at the gate tells me, he was indeed believable in the role. He has just arrived, as you know, and he is ready with his report."

The other man leaned forward, smiled slightly, and said:

"I am Pontius Pilate, Governor of Judea. It was I who ordered your assignment. Where did you find this rabbi, Jesus?"

"I found him in Perea, Excellency..specifically in the city of Gadara where he was guest of honor at a dinner."

"Describe his appearance."

"He was possibly thirty years old, taller than I, and his hair and beard were of a golden color which I thought to be most unusual."(1)

Gaius was startled.

"A blonde Jew?"

"Oh, yes," Pilate interjected. "That's the man. But continue. Did he see you?"

"Well, yes. In order to see and hear what he said, I had to be near him. Even so, I would not have been able to get near on a daily basis over the weeks without the help of one of Jesus' followers, a fellow named Simon."

"So, did you talk with Jesus?"

"No. Even though he saw me, I tried to maintain my anonymity so far as possible. I wanted him to just act naturally as though I was just one of the crowd."

Pilate nodded in understanding and continued:

"How long were you with him?"

"Just about a month."

"I see. And in that time, did he speak against the Emperor or Rome?"

"Never. In fact, before I was there, someone had asked him about paying taxes, and Jesus replied that everyone should give unto Caesar that which was Caesar's."

"Sounds harmless enough."

Did you see any men bearing arms?"

"None."

"Do you think that he could lead an insurrection?"

Cassius wondered whether he could answer so that Pilate would really understand.

"Jesus' manner was always peace-loving and gentle, more concerned with repentance and kindness than any military plan."

Pilate waited.

"You have not answered my question. Could he lead an insurrection?"

Cassius sensed a great urgency in Pilate, a desperate hope for a negative answer. To deny him that would be dangerous, but to avoid the truth would accomplish nothing.

"I have not wished to withhold anything from you, Sir. It is

---

(1) The Archko Volume, "Pilate's Report", Keats Publishing, Inc.

that I just don't know. If I tell you what I saw and heard..those things which I know to be true..perhaps this could be useful to you."

"So?" Pilate queried.

"I attended a dinner in Gadara given for Jesus by a member of their Sanhedrin, a man named Nicodemus. He appeared to be a man of influence and substance. In the course of the events of the dinner, a rather shabby-looking man with dropsy, a deadly disease, asked Jesus to heal him. With nothing more than saying a few words which I was told to be a prayer, The Rabbi held out his hand toward the man, and he was healed. The fatigue and despair which had been so obvious in the fellow left him, and he praised a God at the top of his voice. I didn't understand Jesus' power to heal."

"Yes. Go on," Pilate said dryly.

"I walked with his disciples over a period of weeks, and I saw thousands of people coming from Samaria, Idumea, Greece..I suppose just about everywhere..I saw these people come with little or no food, camping out in the wilderness, and standing for hours just to hear the Rabbi speak. There was something in the way he spoke and the simple things that he said..he called them parables, somehow they were fascinating, and we listened for hours. He had no eloquence like our senators, but the people would not leave. I didn't understand why we were so eager to hear him."

"You too?"

"He didn't know who I was. But yes, I too was glad that I was there."

"Did you see or hear anything more than these parables?"

"Oh, yes. I observed that all of Jesus disciples had no families with them, and I never saw him pay them. That was strange. But the most fascinating thing I have ever seen occurred when we went from Gadara through Jericho and down to Bethany."

Gaius stirred in his chair but said nothing. Pilate leaned forward and watched but remained silent.

Cassius continued:

"I had walked always on the edge of the group which

seemed to follow Jesus wherever he went, and so it was that all of us came into Bethany. Two sisters accosted Jesus there and seemed somehow to hold him responsible for the death of their brother, Lazarus, who had been dead for four days. "

"What did Jesus do?"

"Well, the sisters and their friends, about ten or more of them, all wept; and Jesus did too. By this time, we had come to a cave which had a stone rolled over the opening; and Jesus, pointing in my direction, told us to roll the stone away from the cave. Rather than call attention to myself, I rolled the stone to one side. And, as I stood there, Jesus lifted his head briefly as if in prayer, then turned and pointed his finger directly at the cave opening. He said,`Lazarus, come out!'

"What happened?"

"A man bound in bandages and smelling of cloves struggled to the door. Jesus ordered me to cut his bonds, and I did. "

"And this was the man who had been in the tomb for four days?"

"Yes, it was Lazarus. By some strange power, Jesus had called him to life."

Pilate was restive, turning in his chair and looking out the window.

"And you believe this?"

"Yes. I was there."

"So..what have you told us?"

"I have told you of a man with a strange power, one I can't describe or understand."

"And that is why you haven't answered my question..that is why you don't know whether Jesus could lead an insurrection?"

"I cannot doubt that he could do anything for the reasons that I have told you."

Gaius and Pilate sat quietly for a moment, thinking it over. Then Pilate said softly:

"You did not talk with the Rabbi. Yet you were with him for several weeks. Who or what, if you will, is this Jesus?"

There was nowhere to go, no way to avoid the issue

"I believe him to be as Simon described him. Jesus is the Son of God."

Pilate looked at Gaius to ascertain whether he had any questions to ask, but Gaius shook his head.

"Very well, Centurion. You have provided us with an excellent report. Thank you. You are dismissed."

When Cassius had gone, the two men were silent until Gaius spoke:

"I am so surprised with Voltanus' report. I can't apologize enough.."

"No need for an apology, Tribune. Your man told the truth. In fact, I thought he did remarkably well to understand what he saw."

Gaius' expression reflected his doubt.

"Yes, Tribune, I have no doubt of anything he said."

"But this `Son of God' thing smacks clearly of heresy. The Emperor certainly recognizes no such relationship, least of all with a renegade Jew."

Pilate stood behind his chair, leaning on it as he thought.

"We must not confuse politics and religion. Only you and I have heard these words, and I believe that I can depend upon you to make sure that no one else does hear them. Do you understand me, Alexander?"

"Clearly, Your Excellency. In fact, our young Centurion has already involved himself in another matter which will remove him from our company. His account will not be heard again."

Cassius returned to his quarters with the heavy burden of knowing that he had displeased and embarrassed his commander; and he had with bald clarity stated a truth that Pontius Pilate did not want to hear. So be it. He had done his best.

When he had reached his room, he striped down to his underwear and stretched out on his bed to sleep. He was soon into deep slumber. The door to his room opened without a sound, and a scarred Auxiliary walked in stealthily, opened a drawer and put something into it, and then left. The rhythm of Cassius' breathing never changed. He had slept for two hours when his orderly shook his bed hesitantly.

"Centurion, please wake up, Sir. Unless you move quickly, you will miss dinner."

Cassius dressed quickly and hurried down to the Dining

Room. The food was plain but good, vastly better than his own limited menu of the last several weeks. He ate rapidly so that he really overate, but it did feel wonderful to be full.

He walked briefly in the courtyard and looked up to see the myriad of stars overhead which he had learned to love. He yawned then and knew that there was still more sleep to make up. There were no more duties, nothing more that had to be done just now, and so he returned to his room. He undressed silently and decided that the letter long overdue Portia could be written tomorrow. Pondering the problem of where to begin, he fell asleep.

Heavy pounding on his door startled him, and he sprang from his bed to open it.

"You are Centurion Cassius Voltanus?"

Cassius looked out into the face of a heavy Auxiliary; and behind him, there were three others in full battle dress and carrying spears. He replied:

"You know who I am. What do you want?"

"By the order of Tribune Gaius, your quarters are to be searched. Here are my written orders to search. You will stand aside."

While two of the four stood in front of him the other two began to search through his clothing and luggage. The room was small and the furniture sparse so that the search was over quickly.

Picking up something of gold, the Searcher looked up and said:

"Please dress, Centurion. You will accompany us. This is the stolen item, I'm quite sure; and so the Tribune requires your presence now."

Words would be wasted on these brutes, at least until he had been vindicated by the Tribune. Obviously a dumb mistake.

The five of them marched across the courtyard, mounted two flights of steps and stopped before the Tribune's quarters. With quiet respect, the Auxiliary knocked. Gaius appeared immediately.

"We have your ring, I believe Sir. Will you identify it?"

"Of course. Come in."

141

The old man slipped it over his third finger for which it had been fashioned, looked at it fondly for a moment, and then asked:

"Where did you find it?"

"The ring was among the items of clothing in the top drawer of Centurion Cassius Voltanus' furniture. It had been rolled into his underwear. You have verified that this is the stolen ring, Tribune Gaius?"

"It is." Then looking sharply at Cassius, he said:

"You stand accused of the theft of this ring of Tiberius, fashioned for me and given to me by The Emperor at the Danube.

What is your answer?"

"You know that I did not take it. I have never seen it except on your hand."

"Do you deny that it was found in your possession?"

"No..they found it in my room but.."

"That is all. By the Imperium of My Office, I find you guilty and unworthy of the Roman Citizenship which I conferred originally and which I retract now. Thereby you are no longer an officer but a Greek Auxiliary without rank. You will be imprisoned here at Antonia until a time convenient for punishment."

He turned then and summoned the Guard.

"There is a plain brown tunic in the small room there. It will fit this thief. Remove the uniform which he wears now, and see that he puts on this more suitable garb. Now get him out of here!"

Gaius' cold cruelty had a numbing effect on Cassius. He stared incredulously until prodded by the burly guard.

"Move it, Greek!"

Cassius felt the sharp painful jab in his ribs and moved quickly toward the small room adjacent to Gaius' Office. So much was possible. Was he angry because he had somehow discovered his affair with Portia? Could it be that this was his punishment, dealt so quickly, for having told the truth of Jesus..surely one could call that `treason' if he chose!

After he had laid aside the beautiful uniform of which he had been so proud, he donned the coarse burlap covering which was provided occasionally for prisoners likely to be in detained for a period of time before their execution. He was led then by two guards in front and two behind down the cold stone steps which descended into the dungeon in the lower region of Fortress of Antonia Praetorium. An iron gate was opened before them, then another, and finally Cassius was turned to his left to walk directly into a small cell so situated as to be in constant view of the guard station. The two guards in front stepped aside, and Cassius felt the slap of the flat side of a spear. The impact drove him to the back of the cell. The door clanged shut, and the light of the torches receded, leaving him in almost total darkness.

Some purpose was to be served, he reasoned, surely something more than could be discovered either by his recollection of events or by reasoning. Perhaps Gaius wanted to impress Pontius Pilate with this demonstration of loyalty to the Emperor, and he would be taken out quietly, sent to an outpost somewhere until this Jesus problem was over. Then he could start living again. But where would Portia enter his life again? With these thoughts, he slept.

CHAPTER SIXTEEN

He was awakened with the light of flickering torches and the rough command to get up and follow the guards. He felt dirty and uncomfortable with the thought that he would appear before anyone without a shave. They ascended the same steps that he had walked down hours before..there was no way to mark the time of day until he saw the sunlight. Peculiarly, they returned to the rather sumptuous quarters of Alexander Gaius.

Gaius waved the soldiers out and turned to the puzzled Cassius.

"We have much to discuss, Cassius. Relieve yourself in my bath, clean yourself up, and then you will find a good meal awaiting you."

Gaius himself seemed grey and tired as if he had not slept. His hand trembled as he pointed toward his bath. Cassius was grateful for the hot water available for washing, but the knowledge that his terrible imprisonment was apparently ending was like a reprieve to life itself.

Gaius watched in some pitiful envy as Cassius ate heartily, quickly swallowing the hot cakes and platter of meat before him.

Then, with heavy fatigue, he sat down behind his great desk.

"I will talk with you as man to man. I have never taken shelter behind my rank, and so it will be now. The burden before me is greater than I can carry alone, and peculiarly, I look to you for help."

"How can I help, Sir?"

"I must know. Have you and Portia been lovers while I was away?"

Cassius could not dodge his guilt. He searched desperately for some way to explain it ..not as a betrayal to Gaius..rather as a thing that just happened with nothing else even considered. But how?

"Just tell me the truth."

"Yes, Sir, but it was not as you.."

"Never mind that. 'Yes' will do."

The old man stood then..walked to look to the courtyard below.

As he stood with his back to Cassius, his shoulders drooped; and when he turned back, his face was bathed in tears.

"You have never really known it, because I couldn't really express it. But I have loved you as my son since your father..my old friend..died. I have been proud of you, seeing you become a man worthy and proud to be a Roman Officer." Despite his lost fight for control, Gaius sobbed. "And now.."

"And now, you have taken it all back."

The old man blinked, seeing for the first time that he had used his office as a weapon.

"I have no other choice. Portia is carrying your child, and laughably, it will be thought to be mine."

"Could it not be yours?"

"No, I have been sterile for most of my life, though I never told Portia. No man is proud to be a..farce."

"I see. But what will you do?"

"I will never tell her the truth. She will never know that I know of her unfaithfulness. You see, by never telling her that I was sterile, I lied. And possibly, if I asked her, she probably would lie to me to protect you, to protect my own pride, and lastly of course, to protect the future of that child when it is born. Lies, though they are common among men and perhaps more so among women..lies ruin any life."

Gaius sat down suddenly then, his face ashen. Then, he continued:

"I am sure that you are wondering what my plans are for you."

"Perhaps I know."

"Yes, I will be..I am..forced to have you killed as a common thief. There is no other way. I must murder my own son..and that is what you are to me..I must kill my own son to protect my reputation as a man. My child must never bear the stigma of a bastard. And my wife never to be known as a wanton whore, unfaithful to a man twice er age. I must pay this terrible price, to look every day for the rest of my life on the face of a child

146

looking, quite likely, very much like his father. And I will know for my lifetime that I destroyed the only man that Portia has ever really loved. I alone must know of this. I must bear it all alone in endless dishonor." His military bearing was gone, and Gaius sobbed.

Cassius felt sorrow and compassion for the old man and reached out to him.

"There is another way.."

"`Another' way?"

"You have lied, and you have planned to have me murdered. You have contrived to have Portia's unfaithfulness shielded even from her. You have assumed this terrible burden yourself; and worst of all, my father, you have sinned against the God of Jesus. If you confess to Him.."

"Never!" Gaius roared. "I will never stoop so low as to pray to the god of a Jew!" He had risen from his chair, and his fist crashed down onto the top of his desk.

A questioning look crossed his face then. He clutched his chest, walked a few paces from behind his desk, and fell heavily to the floor. With the first outburst of Gaius' rage, a guard burst into the room with his broadsword in hand. Looking first at Cassius and then to the body of Gaius on the floor, he dropped quickly to one knee and felt for a pulse in the old man's neck. Then, he rolled him over onto his back and looked into his eyes.

"The Tribune is dead," he said. "You could have been charged with his murder except that you are already sentenced to death on a cross as a thief."

By now, two other guards had come into the room, and they escorted Cassius back to his cell.

Portia finished her baby clothes task and went to sit by the bedroom window and look over the fortress wall toward the big round mountain covered with Olive Trees...people here called it the Mount of Olives. It was a peaceful looking place and, indeed it seemed to bring more peace to her. Distantly she heard the knocking at the front door. Heard Lea's voice speaking and a soldierly voice talking. Then silence. She didn't hear her door open or hear Lea come across the room. The first she knew that

Lea was standing at her shoulder, was the warmth of Lea's body near her and, startled she looked up into Lea's tear-stained face.

Portia quickly got to her feet and reach out toward Lea.

"Oh, my dear...what is wrong? What has happened to cause you to cry?"

Lea reached out and pulled Portia to her in a close embrace. She started to speak and could not because she began to sob. Portia patted her lovingly.

"Now, dear Lea...cry it out and then you can talk about it."

Lea reached up and grasped Portia's shoulders and gently eased her back to look in her face. Even through her sobs she spoke.

"Oh, Portia...dear, dear Lady Gaius...it is so awful..but it is the Tribune. Portia...how can I say it..."

Portia staring into her face now, exclaimed -

"Say what, Lea? What about the Tribune? Tell me..tell me."

"Portia - - -the Tribune is dead...." the last word was only a whisper and Portia didn't grasp the truth.

"The Tribune is...what?!"

Quietly but clearly Lea spoke,

"Dead. Lady Gaius he dropped dead in his office. A Centurion came to tell you, but I told him to come back later...that I would tell you."

Portia stared at Lea helplessly as the truth reached her. With a helpless little cry she began to sob. Lea lead her to the bed where she crumpled into a heap, sobbing. Lea sat beside her. Petta opened the door and she also was in tears. Lea motioned her to sit down. Portia's sobs had eased and she sat up.

"He..he hasn't looked well to me....not since we arrived. His color wasn't right...he looked so old...." her tears were silent now.

"Was he sick at the office...did they say?"

"The Centurion, who brought the news, found him in the office. He had apparently collapsed to the floor in some sort of attack and was gone instantly. He didn't suffer."

Portia fell back on the bed.

"I'm glad he didn't suffer." Mopping her eyes she saw Petta

mopping hers and added "I'm sorry for all of us...but don't bother with me for dinner, Petta...I can't eat."

"None of us can." Lea said, then added "The Centurion told us that we should not worry, everything will be taken care of and we will be notified about the funeral -- it'll be military, of course."

Portia stood up...wiped her face dry, smiled weakly at the other two women.

"Military..of course..what else." her voice was a shade hard.

Lea turned sharply and looked at her. Their eyes met in understanding. Lea took a deep breath. Knowing Portia's secret, she realized that her grief was real enough but she was not destroyed by it.

Somehow Portia survived the rigors of the military funeral and the fanfare. In her mind it was more brutal than anything else and she shut her mind away from it even while she witnessed it in its entirety. She was a beautiful and startling figure, admirable in her dignity during the ceremony, though her heart ached for the man she had known since childhood. Sadness moved into her spirit for days to come.

CHAPTER SEVENTEEN

The darkness was unbroken, the stench ongoing, and Cassius neither saw nor heard anything except the occasional clang of the gates when other prisoners were admitted. Water and a tasteless, greasy broth was brought to his cell after some hours, and he assumed that it was night. He slept fitfully, awakening every now and then to be reminded of his death sentence and the ironic thought that the only man who could have given him a reprieve was himself already dead.

It was after several such frightening episodes that he saw a flickering light, torches again, coming down the corridor to his cell. What now? Was he to brought out again and tortured because of Gaius' death?

"You have a visitor, Greek." The Guard's voice was almost friendly. As Cassius stared in disbelief, the sturdy figure of Simon appeared.

"Simon? The Romans would never permit me to have visitors, and least of all, you. How did you do it, and why are you here?"

Cassius heard the friendly chuckle of the fisherman and then felt his powerful hug.

"I just asked to see you, and all of the guards seemed pleased to help me."

"But how?"

"Friend Voltanus, would you believe that you could be here, and Jesus would not know it?"

"I don't know."

"He knew, and by the same power by which he made the blind to see, raised Lazarus from the dead..that same power opened doors for me; and I am here."

"So you are..and God be praised! But why?"

"Your love for Portia and for the baby you'll never see..well, she must be told, and there is no other way for her to know unless I tell her. What would you have me tell her?"

Cassius pondered..what to tell her? It seemed so long ago since he had seen her..could he tell her of his strange assignment and of his discovery of one Jesus called The Christ? The events had taken weeks and intense teaching by Simon for him to comprehend; could he expect Portia to understand?

Simon seemed to read his thoughts.

"She won't understand at first. But I have time. And as God's grace opened your mind and heart, so it will be with Portia. Though she does not yet know it, she will return to Alba; and with her will go a faith like yours. Be of good courage, my son. All will be as He intended, and that long before you ever left Rome."

Cassius was silent with wonder. Then, suddenly the crushing burden of knowing that he was to be crucified..that was lifted and he felt an incredible joy. Coming back to the reality of the Present, he said:

"You are right, Fisherman. There is no way that I can tell her..only you can do that. But I can tell her as you never could that I love her and wish, were it not to be otherwise, that I could be with her for a lifetime. I wish that I could love our child and raise him or her to be like Portia, to laugh in the sunlight and to put glory into love. Tell her that, my friend, though you'll have trouble with the words."

He laughed for the first time in a long, long time. Simon would sound ridiculous! And then tears bathed his cheeks.

"You and I know that there is life beyond here and now..wherever Jesus will be, there will be life. And, from what you have said, that will be a life forever. Though I don't understand it all, I must be a part of that, or you wouldn't be here."

"You are right, my son, though I don't understand either."

The door of the cell opened, and the guard said:

"You must go now. Come with me."

Quickly Simon gathered him again into a powerful hug. And then, Cassius stood alone in the dark as Simon's steps faded into silence.

The darkness and silence seemed to Cassius to be like death without a tomb. All that had meaning had been taken so quickly

152

from him..all within a matter of days. His report which Gaius should have accepted with enthusiastic approval..that was a catastrophe. His hope for reunion with Gaius and another chance just to hear Portia say his name..that too was lost forever. His life, his career..what was he doing here in this stench-filled dungeon? His despair was as dark as the prison around him.

His thoughts were disturbing, frightening. As he thought back on his walk in the wilderness, he remembered that strange moment that Simon called baptism. He had confessed..talked of his sins to a god that he couldn't see and who didn't talk back. Still, there had been a feeling of incredible joy and a light that seemed to come from within himself. This, Simon said, this was prayer. Would it help now..was there a god who cared? And so, once again he talked quietly in the night, again to a god he couldn't see; he prayed. Silently, his panic left him, and there was a strange peace. Cassius slept.

The cell door slammed open and back against the bars.

"Wake up, Greek! Put on your sandals, and come with us!"

Cassius looked up into the grim visage of the guard, a different one this time. His expression was hard and lined with the task before him, set on memories of a hundred scenes like this one. He had heard that this one was a thief, a silly fool who had stolen, of all things, an Emperor's Ring from a Tribune. It didn't matter..another crucifixion, another body rotting in the sun and covered with those green flies which never had their fill.

"Fall in!" He was shoved into place with two guards in front and two behind, and the five of them began a quick ascent of the stairs.

"I wonder how many have left this place, walked up these same stairs and died as I will," Cassius mused.

"Move it, Greek!" admonished the older guard in the rear. In the dim light of early morning, he looked vaguely familiar. Was he one of those transferred from the garrison at Caesarea Philippi? Perhaps Cassius looked familiar to him also, for he looked away, determined that he would feel no weakness in this task before him.

They marched down a cobble-stone street, aware that it seemed that hundreds of people were milling around between the

Praetorium and the Temple, but that was behind them. Cassius was hungry, remembering that his last meal was hours..days even..ago when he had been fed so sumptuously for the last time by that sad old man, Gaius. But hunger would be his least concern, he thought. He tried not to think of the ordeal before him except to hope that it would be soon and out of the way so that ..he could go on living! What a strange thought! Certainly not if these brutal Romans had their way!

Soon they came to a hill which they began to climb in a circuitous path. He looked into its side and saw that it resembled a skull.

"This is Golgotha," the familiar guard said softly He said nothing more, and Cassius wondered if he had heard correctly. The man's voice had broken as if he had been sobbing within himself.

"Strange what one can imagine in a moment life this," Cassius thought.

There! There it was..a rough-hewn post which had a small step at its bottom and then another post fixed at right angles with spikes which jutted out the back..that up three or four feet from the bottom of the first. Both had been stained brown with the blood of countless others before him, and Greek smiled within himself in bizarre humor..surely they could afford a new cross to crucify one as important as Demosthenes or Cassius Voltanus or whoever he was!

The guard at the cross sized him with a practiced eye and saw no reason to adjust the cross-bar up or down.

"Lie down here!" he ordered. The whip in his hand was ready to persuade.

Cassius stretched out on the crude posts, and four rough hands pulled him taut. Held immovable, his wrists and ankles were pierced quickly with long cruel spikes, and two workmen with heavy hammers drove the spikes home into the hard wood. His blood spurted and ran off his arms and legs while the cross was hoisted without delay and dropped into the waiting slot in the ground which was designed to hold its burden until the next victim. The pain which had flashed through him in fierce agony was momentarily intensified a hundred-fold when the post hit bottom, and he blacked out. As he emerged into consciousness again, he was mercifully numbed to his agony, at least long enough to see the mob around him. Another man had been nailed into place just before him, and Cassius was astonished to see a beaten and bleeding Jesus being nailed to a cross between them. It came back to him then; Simon had said that Jesus often spoke of dying on a cross.

Soon Jesus too was in place, and a crowd of jeering scum was calling out to him:

"You were going to raise the temple in three days. Come down, if you can..come down if you are the Son of God!" Their raucous laughter seemed strange in this setting.

Gathered below too was a group of some well-dressed Jews..Pharisees, no doubt, now glad to see this would-be rabbi getting his punishment. One strident voice emerged, saying:

"He saved others, but he can't save himself! He's the King of Israel. Let him come down from the cross, and we'll believe in him!"

Then another voice wafted up to him,

"He trusted in God. Let God rescue him now if he wants him for he said `I am The Son of God'." And there was a rippling, comfortable laughter with the quenching of vengeance sought and long overdue.

The ache within Cassius began to grow, to move in from all side, and to become almost unendurable agony. On the other side of Jesus, the thief called out in a raspy voice:

"Hey, Rabbi! Aren't you the Christ? Save yourself and save us!" And he laughed, a wild peal from the tattered edge of delirium.

Cassius tried to shift his weight, to ease the burden which threatened to burst his chest, but the spikes exerted their own vicious torture.

"Don't you fear God?" he called. "We deserve this, but this man has done no wrong."

From the grey areas before him and what seemed to be a cloud on which he was floating, Cassius said:

"Lord, remember me when you come into your kingdom!"

Then, from his left, for the last time, there came the rich full baritone of The Christ:

"Truly, today, you will be with me in Paradise."

Time had passed unnoticed and unending until from the dimness of his consciousness, Cassius saw that it was growing dark, pitch black. He wondered whether Portia....and then the Earth shook violently. The ear-splitting crash of thunder blasted the sky.

But Cassius heard none of it, nor did he see it. He moved swiftly through a tunnel, oblivious to all pain except for the last dim agony when his legs were broken. Then before him seeming to await his arrival, there was glorious white light.

Was this Paradise?

CHAPTER EIGHTEEN

Portia felt as though she were living in animation, that life had suddenly become unreal and intangible. Gaius` body had been cremated only five days ago and, while she had been treated with recognition and respect by the Garrison

Tribune of Jerusalem and someone named Publius who said that he represented Governor Pontius Pilate, these by no means assuaged her concern with her future and that of her household. How were they to eat, pay rent on this lovely little home or, was it a benefit provided by Rome for them? Death simply had not been considered as a possibility. She was so bewildered with it all. Awhile back she had felt she had `grown up'! She hadn't known the meaning of the word. She was finding out!

Though she had not even the faintest semblance of appetite, she knew that she must maintain nutrition for the baby inside. She had just settled down to a bowl of fruit and fresh bread when Lea announced,

"A messenger has just arrived and requests seeing you. He is waiting in the All Purpose room.

"A messenger? From whom?"

"He announced himself as Publius from the office of Pontius Pilate, Governor of Judea."

"Oh, yes. I did meet him earlier. I guess he needs to know something. Show him to the All Purpose room, Lea."

She knew that she looked less than her best, but she summoned what she hoped would pass for the dignity of a Tribune's widow, and walked into the All Purpose room where he waited.

"Good day, Publius. May I help you?" she said simply

"And good day to you, Lady Gaius. His Excellency has been much concerned with your welfare, but this has been the first opportunity to extend his respects. He has directed me to make myself available as part of your household as you need me, and then asked that you visit with him the day after tomorrow.

His day begins at the tenth hour. Will that be acceptable to you?

"Yes, of course. But I don't know where."

"I shall be pleased to escort you, Lady Gaius."

"I see."

"And I'm not sure that you are aware of it, but this villa is yours with your staff as long as you need it. I have arranged that food will be delivered. If I err in the provisions made, please change the order to your liking."

"How kind of you. And for travel, for getting around in this strange city of Jerusalem?"

"That too will be taken care of. But I'm sure that the Governor will want to explain just what provisions have been made for you and your servants. Will you wish to go out today, or is there anything needed for your comfort now?"

"No, in both cases, Publius. Please tell the Governor that I shall be there as he has invited."

Publius left, and Portia was left again with her thoughts and the persisting hope that Cassius would come back to make her life livable again. At least now, she dare think of him without fear.

The Sun had begun its descent in the West, and the shadows had lengthened, when Lea announced yet another visitor.

"Who this time, Lea?"

"He is a rather rough looking man named Simon."

"Is he also part of the government?"

"No..no, he is dressed much like the travelers we saw and he did not say just what he wanted."

"I think not. I am not feeling well, and I don't feel up to seeing strangers without its being necessary."

Lea turned and walked out, prepared to dismiss the caller.

But shortly thereafter, she came aback and in obvious excitement said,

"He says that he has a message from Cassius!"

For the first time in weeks, Portia felt relief and joy. Hurrying out to the All Purpose room again, she said,

"I am Lady Gaius. What message do you have for me?"

Simon stood, conditioned for a lifetime to be respectful of the affluent.

"I am Simon, Lady Gaius. The message and all of the information that I have for you comes from Cassius, and they are all words of tender intimacy."

"He is not here? Where is he? Why is he not here to speak for himself?"

The lines in Simon's face seemed to deepen, and his shoulders drooped with dread as he considered the terrible account that he must give her.

"Please sit down."

She resented his direction, but she remembered the occasionally stern discipline of Gaius. She sat..and waited. Simon turned briefly away, to gather his thoughts, and then he said, "Before your husband died, he learned that you and Cassius were lovers, and he had that fine young man crucified as a thief. Cassius is dead."

The normal sounds were suddenly gone, and she could only see as from a long way off. She stood and then she screamed in wild frenzied grief. She collapsed and would have fallen from the chair, but Simon moved to support her and when she awakened, he was holding her hand. She was oddly at peace. Lea was standing in back of Simon in consternation, but Portia signaled that she was all right.

"Please tell me what happened."

"There is so much to tell, and I know that it is vitally important that you understand. You can't absorb it all today. But this much you must know now...this very instant. Your magnificent Centurion was with me in the wilderness of Perea and later in Bethany. He told me of his great love for you. His last message, sent from the prison here in the Praetorium, was that he loved you and his baby."

"He knew that it was his baby?"

"Yes."

"But how? I wasn't even sure myself until you told me just now."

"That, Dear Lady, is part of the great good news that I have for you. But no more for today. You must rest. Then, you must be patient, for I shall be away for a matter of weeks. But we have a great friend here in your house, and that is Publius.

159

He will come, and he will go; for we have much for him to do. Pilate believes that he is <u>his</u> servant, and he is that. But he has a far greater role to play. Keep in touch with him; and one day before long, you will begin a wonderful new life."

Portia stared at Simon for a long moment.

"Do you know, I find all of this so strange quite possibly because of you. I don't know you at all, but I could believe that my life..yes even <u>our</u> lives would be safe with you."

Simon's task had been done, the essential message delivered.

"Good night, Lady Gaius. Peace be with you."

Simon left then, as if he had every right to come and go as he wished. And Portia wondered through her deluge of sorrow...who was this man? And how could he know?

The Moment came..the time to meet with that great man who had been so kind in his address at Gaius' funeral. Portia was not worldly-wise, but she had observed that men and their words were not always necessarily consistent. What was he really like?

"I am ready when you are, Lady Gaius."

Publius' peremptory comment prompted her to the moment, and she replied:

"I am ready."

She felt just a bit out of character as if she had inherited some of Gaius' mantle. It was not her liking, but meeting reality at this moment required mature firmness that she remembered having seen in older women..yes, widows as she recalled, women in her situation.

"You may need to watch these steps, Lady Gaius. In this light, they can be deceptive."

Did he think her to be so doddery that she couldn't see the edge of the steps? With that flip thought, she stumbled, and his hand steadied her.

"I see what you mean."

She couldn't know, of course, but her venerable Gaius had walked up these same steps, through the same doors, and into the elegance of Pilate's home only a few weeks ago.

They continued down the elegant corridor, now delightfully cool on a warming June morning, and then into an exquisite room clearly furnished for comfort but quietly beautiful with statues of Tiberius, Augustus Caesar, and one or two other busts of the Greats of Rome. A slender lady, dressed simply in black and with blonde hair coifed carefully close to her head, stepped forward and extended her hand.

"Lady Gaius, I am Andelia Pilate. Welcome to our home."

Portia was so pleased with Pilate's tact. He must have known of a woman's apprehension in dealing with him or any other man at such a horrible time. To be greeted by his wife in his own home was a gracious gesture. Women she understood, but most men had, in one way or another, resembled the no-nonsense manner of Gaius.

Andelia's voice brought her back to the present.

"And how are you doing, My Dear? Are you able yet to find yourself....at least enough to begin to put your life back together again?"

Portia smiled slightly

"Not exactly, Lady Pilate. Daily living has not yet taken on any semblance of reality. I wake with too much of the world of dreams getting tangled with memory...I'm not sure which is which."

As Portia watched the face of Andelia Pilate and saw that the comment had not registered as well as it might. She added:

"Do you know what I mean?"

As if drawn back from somewhere else in her thinking, Pilate's wife responded with an almost imperceptible start.

"Oh, yes..yes, I do know what you mean. I, too, find myself sometimes struggling with dreams that seem of themselves to have a kind of permanence.."

Pilate himself had entered the room unnoticed by either and announced himself abruptly to end the course of conversation already in disturbing areas.

"Lady Gaius, I am Pontius Pilate. Thank you for having taken time to visit with us today. I should have gotten to you sooner, but.."

Strange that such an urbane man would leave his statement in an awkward ending.

"Oh, I do understand, Excellency. And I have wanted for

nothing. In fact, I have been grateful that, after the catastrophe of Gaius's sudden death, I had the time to begin to find myself again. And your Publius has been so considerate."

How she hated these words which so beat about the bush, but this was Rome again, if not in fact, at least in essence.

He gestured toward one of the great chairs and seated himself at a small desk. Andelia sat down to Pilate's left, while Portia's chair was more closely positioned near the center of his desk.

"First, Lady Gaius, you know that I have tendered my condolences. Further, I am told that there is a wonderful aspect of this awful tragedy. You are to have a baby! When is the child to be born?"

Portia smiled with the thought that they were separated so far apart in social structure but so bound together inexorably in the processes of life.

"Dr. Tibius tells me that I have yet another three months to wait...quite possibly in late September or early October."

Pilate was politely interested, but only politely. It was so subtle but ever so sure that something bothered him. And so, with no more pretense in that which never interested men anyway, he pushed the discussion to matters immediately at hand.

"You may wish to remain here in Jerusalem, or it may be that you would prefer to return to Rome. At any rate, in my profound admiration and respect for your gallant husband whose exploits are known even to Tiberius himself. In those we open Jerusalem to you. Your villa is yours for as long as you wish to stay. Your food will be delivered fresh daily to your door, and Publius will be your immediate access to our assistance."

Words, words, words! How she hated them! The closely observant Pilate paused and asked:

"Is there something wrong, Lady Gaius?"

"Oh, no, Your Excellency! I am so overcome with your generosity.."

"Not `generosity', Lady Gaius. Let us say that it is a part payment of our debt to the gallantry of Alexander Gaius. I am so personally indebted to him.."

"May I ask in what way, Sir? My husband left so quickly upon receipt of your orders to report to you here in Jerusalem that I never really understood his duties."

Pilate shifted in his chair, crossed one leg over the other, and looked out the window as if to recollect more clearly the events at hand.

"I called the Tribune to Jerusalem to counsel me. He suggested brilliantly that we slip a spy into the Jesus group, someone to report back to us. Not only did he originate the brilliant plan, but he also sent a young Centurion named Voltanus into that mission disguised as a Jew, one following this rabbi in his ramblings out there in the wilderness which have seemed to be his preferred habitat."

"And did my husband's plan help you to find out about the rabbi?"

Pilate glanced quickly at his wife and back again to Portia, hoping that he could answer without opening a subject of private volatility.

"We have had a dangerous condition among the peoples of this region for some time, Lady Gaius. In the time just passed, indeed the day following your husband's sudden demise, the Jews observed Passover. And for at least the three years before that, there has been a growing unrest among them, fomented largely by a rustic rabbi named Jesus of Nazareth. We suspected that the uprising which we have expected for some time..we thought that this Jesus might be organizing such an uprising."

Sensing a movement to her right, Portia saw that Pilate's wife, still seated in her chair, glistened as if bathed in perspiration.

"So what did you learn?"

Pilate glanced sharply at Portia. Then he continued.

"The young Centurion returned with an interesting report. He felt that the rabbi was harmless, but your husband and I comprehended that he would, in a short time, undermine his own people's government, the Sanhedrin, and he presented a very grave threat to the Emperor himself."

"And the young Centurion?"

"That was entirely a military matter which I left to your

husband's decision. I have not heard further of his assignment. For our part, we recognized the danger in this Jesus, the rabbi. His own people had him executed."

Abruptly Andelia Pilate made a strangled little cry and left the room quickly. Pilate glanced up at his wife's sudden exit and sought some means by which he could cover his embarrassment. He stood, obviously unsettled with their own private discord, and asked:

"And are you planning to stay with us, Lady Gaius?"

"Thank you for your generosity, Governor.   Yes, I plan to be here at least until the delivery of our baby.."

"Yes, yes, of course. Now Publius will see you to your home. Rome is eternally in your debt."

Pilate raised his hand, an expected signal to Publius, and Portia was escorted quickly from the mansion. The meeting had not gone well, but it was not of her doing. At least, the necessities were taken care of. But his calloused dismissal of Cassius was almost certainly a thinly disguised lie, and Portia hoped that Andelia Pilate had the power to humble him. Men! She boiled with anger even though her unanswered questions of Cassius haunted her...Oh, how could Gaius ever have done such a terrible thing? Publius saw her to the little house and after ascertaining that there was no need of his services for the rest of the day, he departed.

Standing beside the fountain, staring into the lily pond, she looked at herself. Her mind raced back over the preceding days and then, again, over this day's meeting with Pilate...hearing his words,"...that was entirely a military matter which I left to your husband's decision."

The truth of that decision had ripped a hole in her heart and soul. Gaius' death had saddened her and had bequeathed her a great deal of worry and concern over the future. With the truth of Simon's words and of Pilate`s today, one thing stood out. Gaius had murdered Cassius. Grief for Gaius no longer existed. Quite suddenly she loathed the sound of the name!

Lea came from the house toward her.

"Are you all right, Portia?"

Looking up at her friend with wet eyes, Portia smiled

weakly.

"Yes. I do have a confirmation of that which Publius told me.

We are assured of living here as long as we like and of all food. We can also expect transportation if we need it and have Publius at our beck and call. Now, that is all to the good would you not agree?"

"Oh, wonderful, Portia. Did you find out anything else?"

"Yes. It was confirmed that Gaius murdered Cassius."

Portia had spoken so coldly and with a voice so void of feeling that Lea gasped. She moved quickly to Portia,

"Oh, Portia...that is dreadful."

Portia turned to her, arms outstretched, and as Lea embraced her she began to sob...in genuine grief for the man she had truly loved.

They both sat down on the edge of the fountain and finally Portia's tears ran dry.

"Lea, I am cried out. But there is no sadness in me any longer for Alexander. He is gone and I am blessed. I can now get on with putting me back together for this baby."

Petta had been watching for a long time from the back doorway and evening was settling down as they stood and made their way into the house. She shook her head sadly and went into the kitchen to await Lea as to what to do about supper.

Portia went to her room early and sat in her chair by the window and let her mind look into the future. Until baby came she would stay here, of course. Dr. Tibius would tell her when she could travel. At that point she would request request transportation to Caesarea and approved passage on a ship back to Rome. From there it would be home to Alba, of course. What to do was no problem, but the passage of time and the need to recover from the horror of this new grief would take all her strength and will power.

A couple of days later the house began to "move in on her" and she asked Lea if it would be proper for them to leave the living area surrounding the Fortress and go into the City. Lea was excited with the prospect because she needed to find her way around also.

The two of them set out afoot one day to "see the City", and when they returned that night, they had to laugh at their attempt. They never could walk and see the city in several days let alone one. It was sprawling and the streets had to be climbed or gone down, for everything was built the way the land rolled. Whatever the city was, it was a beautiful place.

Again, Lea and Portia wandered out onto the streets of the ancient city of Jerusalem, aware that to some, they were conspicuous; but she was Lady Gaius, a widow and not one now to be concerned with the opinions of the men of various cultures for whom women in general were chattel. They roamed the streets, visited the shops of their choice, and returned at night with the tired but satisfied feeling of adventurers learning about a new land, the land of Hebrews. The vast temple, occupying the highest part of the entire city, was of gleaming limestone 180 ft long, 90 ft. high with bronze pillars 40 ft high flanking the east entrance. Later, Publius described the interior with its walls covered with hand-carved paneling and the cypress flooring. Not even an inch of stone was exposed. Absolutely beautiful. The Temple courtyard bustled with activity. Men with bushy beards hustled along in voluble exchange with others who looked very much as they did, while beggars sat pathetically by the great pillars through which the throngs were passing. One heard the cooing of doves and the bleating of lambs in their pens as they awaited their moments of slaughter. What a strange concatenation of sounds and people were involved in this business of worship!

Portia found herself more amused than enchanted, but the beauty of the stones, the elegance of Grecian architecture, were astounding. The day they visited the Upper City where the wealthy citizens lived, was almost unbelievable. It was Rome all over again -- the same architecture and the same elegance. One couldn't believe it was in Jerusalem. At the end of that day, Portia turned to Lea,

"No more. I have seen enough of Jerusalem. As fascinating as it is, I am homesick. I want to stay in our own little house and garden until baby comes and then run home to Alba."

"Oh, but, Portia, what will I do without you....?"

"You have Dan, Lea. I will have a wee baby, a fatherless baby. I can't stay here."

"I am sorry, Portia...I didn't mean - -"

"No, Lea, I know that you didn't. That's the way it is, that's all."

Now beginning her seventh month of pregnancy, Portia felt concern with her increasing girth; and she found it difficult to maintain the personal cleanliness which had always been of an inward sense of pride. Dr. Tibius had come, as she had asked, and found that both mother and child were indeed doing well, though he expressed a gentle concern that Portia was slightly anemic and a few pounds underweight.

"Your child is healthy, Lady Gaius. But he or she will not progress as well after birth if you deny him nutrition now."

His lecture continued and she listened patiently, knowing as she did that such remonstrances of an older man was in its own way reassuring, a kind of fatherly love in another form.

"Yes, Dr. Tibius, I do understand. And Lea will help me to remember."

She had just finished when Lea announced that Publius had just entered the house in great excitement.

"You must come now..as soon as possible, Lady Gaius! Simon has not summoned you, though I know that he would. But a most awesome thing is happening . Please come quickly!"

Portia slipped hurriedly into her clothes and followed the greatly agitated Publius. It was yet fairly early in the morning, only a bit after nine o'clock, and there were as yet few people about in the streets. Publius and Portia approached a fairly large two-story building only a sort distance from the Temple when they heard a sound like the rush of wind, but the trees overhead were not moving.

"What is that sound, Publius?"

"I don't know, Lady Gaius. I only know that we have been praying and worshiping in this building, and now.."

His voice trailed off as lights flickered through the building, and excited voices were heard in obvious shouts of praise. Portia looked at Publius questioningly, but he just shook his head. He did not understand. Suddenly the sound of footsteps - many

167

footsteps, running down steps was heard. Shortly, men burst forth from the building. Individually, they went up to people in the streets and began talking to them. There were many nationalities in Jerusalem and, mysteriously, even to the men themselves who spoke to others, they spoke in a language which that person would understand. The greatest mystery was to the unlettered Galileans themselves who had been in the house, for they did not know the languages they spoke or understand how they chose to speak to people who did. They were proclaiming the good news about Jesus in many tongues. One came up to Publius and Portia and began, in the elegant Latin spoken in Rome, to proclaim the glory of Jesus. He seemed to be speaking to Publius, but his eyes were fastened on Portia.

She listened, bewildered and fascinated -- wondering if what he said was in any way related to Simon, who had promised to tell her so much more. Suddenly then, the speaker turned and approached a black-skinned man across the street by the Temple wall. Again, he spoke rapidly but now in a completely different tongue.

Portia looked around and saw that hundreds of people were being spoken too and that hundreds were also kneeling and with hands reaching heavenward, were seeming to praise God...each in his own native tongue! It was totally bewildering.

Portia's eyes settled on the doorway through which the men had come. Simon stood there...a glowing figure with face turned heavenward. She was transfixed. Simon turned toward her, lifted his arm and pointed in the direction of her house -- nodded ever so slightly. Portia understood.

"I must go home, Publius. Simon will talk to me there."

"Let us go." he answered, in a voice filled with awe.

He took her arm, and they hurried in the direction from which they had come.

They reached the little courtyard and she turned to Publius, standing at the gate.

"Do you need anything?" he seemed to be whispering and she did understand that, for when she said:

"No, thank you." her voice whispered her reply.

They smiled at each other in understanding and then he was

gone.

Portia dropped down to sit on the edge of the fountain, and wept. Her tears washed her spirit, for suddenly there was a great peace and sense of wonder that she simply did not understand. The child within her fluttered and was quiet, as it too rested.

Later, that same day, Simon came.

As Portia walked toward the library of her villa to meet Simon, she reflected on a phenomenon, that of being "under a spell". Being with Cassius had always had the effect of just turning even the most ordinary event into an experience tipped with ecstasy. Being with Simon was something like that only very different. Being with him was like being home with a most wonderful friend.

"Hello, Simon. I'm so glad to see you." Her tears were always so near the surface in his presence, because he had been so close to Cassius.

"And peace to you, Lady Gaius." Strange comment, she thought. And then she noticed that Simon seemed almost incandescent..a glow and a power emanated from him. He continued:

"I saw you on the street today, this most wonderful of days. Did you understand what you were seeing?"

"No, Simon I did not. I wondered whether anyone understood today. But what did you mean by `most wonderful of days'?"

"Today was the coming together of prophecies hundreds of years old. But to explain it to you in this way would be like beginning a story for you and starting in the middle."

"Tell me, Simon, before you begin..would Cassius have been a part of this?"

"Oh, yes. In fact, he is very much a part of it. But let me begin with telling you as I told him of Abram and his wife Sara.."

And so Simon told the story simply but with captivating eloquence. He paced quietly up and down the room and told the marvelous story of a loving God, Yahweh, and his rebellious children, the Jews. The prophets of the Old Testament were as vivid in his memory as if it were yesterday, and he chuckled

169

ruefully as he recalled an embarrassing moment.

"Why are you laughing, Simon?"

"Well, I was there on Mt. Tabor with Jesus when Elijah and Moses came, and I saw them. I wanted to do something useful, and so I offered to build a shelter for them! Imagine! But I digress.."

Lea showed up in the doorway, expecting to prepare food, but Portia waved her away.

The shadows of evening came, and Publius slipped quietly into the room to light the candles. Simon seemed then to come back from his wonderful story into the present.

"You are tired, Portia," he stated simply. And she was so pleased that the formalities had been lost somewhere. They were friends.

"Yes, Simon. I am. But oh, how I wish that I could have been there with you and Cassius to meet Jesus!"

"Would you like to know him, now that you understand?"

"I would give anything.."

"And so you will. Perhaps somewhere, possibly not even long from now, that may be required. But for now..as Cassius did, would you like your sins forgiven and to be born again into this new life?"

Shame and guilt had been shoved back in her mind, but they burst forward now in a torrent of tears.

"Oh, yes. Oh yes..if only I could."

And so there, in the fountain and pool in her own villa, Portia was baptized. The Glory of The Lord filled her soul. While she was yet rejoicing, Simon slipped out into the night.

Slowly Portia became aware of herself -- the patio -- the stillness. Looking around she saw that Simon had left. How long had she stood here with her arms outstretched? She smiled contentedly, feeling a newness within herself. The child stirred within her and her hands stroked her belly. She laughed softly.

Turning toward the house she tip-toed inside, reaching her room without anyone knowing she had left the patio. By the window with her face turned up to the stars, her thoughts filled with memories of Cassius and their love of less than a year ago. Not long ago, really -- but it seemed such a long time. A strange feeling of being alone, so very alone, closed her throat and brought tears to her eyes. At that very moment, the child within her moved, assuring her she was not alone.She never understood the fullness of that moment, really -- for it was then that she took charge of her life. When she arose the next morning she was at peace and in control of the future, with plans for what she was to do quite settled within her. It was all so simple, really. After the baby's arrival she would go home to Alba. The thing to do was get ready for the trip and arrange now for the travel plans.

As much as some things could change, nothing would change her determination for their future -- hers and her baby's.

THE END

There follows here, an expository of the organization of the Roman Army during biblical times, within which time this story is written. We are indebted to Quennells's "Everyday Life In Roman And Anglo Saxon Times" for this information

The Roman Army was divided into Legions and Auxiliaries...the former being the descendants of the early citizens and the farmers, who left the plough to fight. Auxiliaries were recruited from subject peoples.

A Legion was known by a number (such as First, Second, Third, etc.) and could equal from 3000 to 6000 heavy infantry, foot soldiers, with 120 riders for dispatches and scouting. It was commanded by a Senator, nominated by the Emperor as commander-in-chief of a specific Legion, and was known as Legatus Augusti Legionis. There were six military Tribunes of high social rank; 60

Centurions who equaled Majors and Captains and were promoted from the ranks and other inferior officers. Legionaries served with the colors for twenty years and received a bounty and land upon discharge.

Auxiliaries were divided into infantry cohorts...(300 to 600 men or men equal to one tenth of the size of the Legion to which attached). Each Cohort was commanded by an Officer or, Tribune, in charge of the section or department of the Legion to which the Auxiliaries were assigned. Their pay was less than that of the Legionaries and their service was longer. Upon discharge they received Roman Citizenship."

The Bibliography

FOLK AND FESTIVALS (Costumes of the World)
    By: R. Turner Wilcox

A HISTORY OF JEWISH COSTUMES
    By: Alfred Rubens

GEMS
    By: Mab Wilson

EVERYDAY LIFE IN ROMAN AND ANGLO-SAXON
TIMES
    By: Margaret & C.H.B Quennell

ROME
    By: Moses Hadas and Editors..Time-Life Books

THE HOLY BIBLE
    New International Version

SPIRIT FILLED LIFE BIBLE
    General Editor: J.W.Hayford, Litt.D.

Old Testament Editor:
    Sam Middlebrook, D.Min.

New Testament Editor:
    Jerry Horner, TH.D.

EVERYDAY LIFE IN BIBLE TIMES
    (Excerpts) Nat'l Geographic

LIFE IN NEW TESTAMENT TIMES
    By: A. C. Bouquet

JESUS, An Historian's Review of The Gospels,
   By: Michael Grant

JESUS, His Life and Times
   Published by Fleming H. Revell Co.
                    (The Genesis Project, Inc.)

GREAT PEOPLE OF THE BIBLE AND HOW THEY LIVED
   Reader's Digest Association, Inc.
   W/Acknowledgments:G.Ernest Wright,
   Rev.Fr.Stephan J.Hartdegen,OFM,
   James Pritchard, Nadum M. Sarna

THE NARRATED BIBLE
   1984 By: Harvest House Publishers

THE CHRONOLOGICAL BIBLE
   Edited by: Edward Reese   (Reese Religious Research)

THE CHRONOLOGY OF THE BIBLE
   By: Frank R. Klassen

ATLAS OF THE BIBLE
   Pub. Readers Digest

   Editor: Joseph Gardner..Research Editors,
   Monica Borrowman & Mary Jane Hodges

Board of Consultants: Edward F.   Campbell,Jr, Rev. Stephen
Hartdegan, Nahum N. Sarna, etc.

ALSO

   "THE ARCHKO VOLUME or The Archeological Writings
of the Sanhedrin & Talmud of the Jews "
   (These are the Official Documents made in these Courts in
the Days   of Jesus Christ,   translated by Drs. McIntosh and
Twyman   of   the   Antiquarian   Lodge,   Genoa,   Italy,   from

Manuscripts in Constantinople and the records of the Senatorial Docket taken from the Vatican at Rome.

About the Author

Shirley Ricks worked for thirty years in the Motion Picture Industry and raised two children and finished college before she could turn to her one true love, writing. Her greatest hope now is that you will enjoy reading her favorite story as much as she enjoyed writing it.

CPSIA information can be obtained
at www.ICGtesting.com
Printed in the USA
FSOW03n1213220916
25277FS